Character list

Lex- Main character

Jessica- Lexy's Best friend

Latoya- Lexy's big sis

Linsey-Paul's wifey

Paul- Cheating husband

John-bestie of Paul

Milton jay- cartel boss

Ms. Amber rice- nurse for Milton

Rocky -Paul's bottom bitch

The get back

Just a short Intro

This story is a story about a man who had to have too much, belonged to everybody, and no one at all. But all the women in this story are willing to die for him or over him. He was sexy and willing to do whatever for the cheddar. He starts out true to his self but the switch up causes a lot of trouble and rivalry amongst his lovers and friends. When you promise to much and don't deliver its best to keep your eyes open.

Most men want the cake and to eat it too. Who wouldn't? This story takes you through the struggles of loving an all women man and what could happen if a change isn't made. The women in this story are not all innocent either. They lie and keep secrets at whatever cost. Life is full of lessons and these characters are about to learn some.

Lexy Prologue

My mother made sure I was tough and ready for a cruel world. I know she loved me and only gave me what was in her mind, what was best for me. My parents were not around much and when they were there were fighting with someone, something, or each other. I know we had dinner, but I can't cook and don't remember anyone cooking, or a meal all together. I had no real love at home, and I knew the world was not going to offer me any either. I had to learn that lesson the hard way. I knew I was a Star just waiting to be pushed to the next level and I would do what it took to keep my crown facing up right. That is why I cannot keep a friend or family member close; it always ends in disappointment. I learned at an early age from my older sister, all you needed was some dirt on the other person and you held all the power. Not knowing the dirty shit people were into was a big no in this world. The more you knew on someone the better. You must always keep the upper hand so you can't take a major Loss. Leaving my guard down was not an option. Taught to always be on the defense. I do know in my own experiences; you catch more flies with honey and being too sweet to eat. I am a chameleon in my mind. I can always change my colors and adapt.

For the first time in a while things were looking up for me but when my sister ran away my life was standing still. I missed her so much, but I was also hurt she could say fuck me too and just leave. She understands the pain and the hurt that came with this house. I don't get how she could just leave me here to deal with it alone. After the many things my mom did, we vowed to never leave each other. I needed her but she damn sure needed me. She wasn't right in her mind without me, and I could not be without her. I told myself I was going to find my sister and hit a lick that would set us up until we could figure out what we were going to accomplish in this world. I was not going to be the same as my parents. The cycle had to end here. All I had at this moment was my good looks and my body. I watched my peoples from an early age get the money using charm and good looks so I was not clueless. I knew how to dance and finesse. If I kept my head on straight, I was setup to make more than enough money and connections. I just needed to get the attention of the right guy or girl. Get a team of chic's ready to get this money. Then I can put a real plan together. That's all I cared about, and this was going to be a ride to remember. This story is not long but it's about some real ass people doing real things. It's a gangster world we live in. Some live by revenge and its one of the worst sins. Play the game to win Just don't play over the people you win with.

Linsey Aka WIFEY

I always saw my marriage as something to be proud of. I saw my family as something to be proud of too. But something wasn't right in my life anymore and I just can't put my finger on why. What the hell happened? How did I and my husband get at this place? Deep down I knew it was me. No matter what little arguments we have or how long between sex sessions, I knew I was the problem. My dream had always been to run my parents rare bird business. I had worked there since high school and was content to spend my life working up to my father's image. As I got closer to the interworking of the business, I learned the hard truth. My family was the right-hand man to the mafia, and I couldn't tell my husband or family. I couldn't risk their safety. My life was a lie. I have always been a hard worker and followed the rules to a T. That is why this life I was living didn't even seem to belong to me.

I was working in finance when my father got sick and needed constant care. I wasn't sure what he was doing at the time, but I wanted no parts, but seeing him in pain was too much for me to handle. How was he going to keep everything going? Someone had to keep my family afloat. If I didn't step up how would my poor mother be in the business? I had to help. From that day forward I have been laundering drug money. Hiding it from my family. I hated lying to my kids about my day. Being absent at games and recitals through the years. Most days I had the nanny filling in for me or making sure we all had what we needed. Before I started helping my dad, I was always home. outside of my nine to five jobs at the company, I was home being wifey. I made good money. My husband also worked alongside me at the company, so we were in a good financial state. I did not need to do anything extra to take me away from my home, but I was loyal to the family.

Did my best to keep my husband and my children happy and safe. After all these years I was tired of the lies and wanted just a normal marriage. No hiding or leaving your life in your trunk at night. Every so often I feel like ill crack under all the pressure. No friends or close family. My life didn't allow for it. I would tell my hubby I was out with friends or a little birthday party, but it was always something he just couldn't be a part of.

I knew my dad participated in something not necessarily legal, but I never had to deal with that at all and neither did our family I assumed. I never in a million years guessed that our entire family legacy was based on dirty money. My dad asked me to run the company some years back I declined and in a few weeks' time he had fallen ill. The moment I started doing all the jobs and running things for my dad's company that the red flags showed up all over. None of the receipts or ledgers matched. We were buying all kinds of things not needed in the building for research of birds or seeds. The people that came and went from the office were a bit odd and scary to say the least.

One night I was there late sorting packages and putting labels on the boxes. This was not my job but the shipping department was getting behind. I was told to never open said boxes. I was to make sure to label and sort them according to zip code. I asked the men to load the pallets and get the trucks loaded up and I saw a few men going in one of the crates. I walked to the office and zoomed in with the cameras on the men and what they were doing. No sooner than I could pick up my phone, three men came up behind them. They covered their heads with black bags and took a kill shot to the head. They threw the bodies in the back of a red pick-up and sped off. In shock at what I saw. I did not need to open the box to know it was not rare bird seeds I was shipping. I looked at myself in the mirror and hated myself for what I saw. For not just going to my mother and putting a stop to it but I didn't want to know anything more. Comping out and I was honest with myself about that. I just wanted to keep my head down and ignore it all. I knew one day all of this would boil over inside me, but today I just wanted to be a ghost.

I had more than enough money coming in, so I did not ask any questions and did what was expected, and what I was told. A few months after the incident I felt good again. I wasn't sure what had happened, but I knew I was on the good side of things. I wasn't going to be involved in any more than I needed to be. I knew my lane and I was staying in it. I know what I saw that night, but I knew I design bird seeds and the best way to feed over one hundred different birds in our city. Best part of our marketing team too.

After I cried and complained a bit. I decided to embrace my new job title and focus on getting a new guy. Blocked out anything I saw that night and anything that others were saying. I was the best at the company. Could do every job in the building down to our warehouse. So, at this point in my life, I'm going to get some fun. I already had my eyes set on a man I was going to try and marry. He was so fine, and he was half black, or native, I didn't care I just love some soulful dick. The way my last man could flip me over and pound my pussy. Who in their right mind would want a boring man after that? I love my people, but I swear I was a black woman stuck in a white woman's body. I had curves and soul that never quite fit in with my family or friends. Hair was curly and wild. I looked like the kid someone invited over to the party in every family photo. My mother cooked and I was giving pointers by age eight. Everything I eat must have spicy sauce on it and be seasoned with meat. Can you imagine me as a kid with all the other white kids? Hated cookouts and potlucks. At every gathering I was the different girl. It was hard knock life at school, but I would not change any part of me. Just going to get a man who could manage it and except me for me. I've been really feeling this guy a saw a few times around town, and I think he fits my speed. When I saw him leave my block, I asked a few people in the bar about him. I couldn't get any one to say one bad word, but they all begged me to leave him alone. A nice girl can get messed up trying to hang with him. Now it was official I was not going to let anything keep me from Paul Jones. It is like you tell me something is taboo and now It becomes a goal.

I saw him at a café in a not so good part of town. I was dropping off a package for pops when I saw him in the alley-way smoking. He smiled at me and asked if I wanted to hit his smoke. Walked over to him and accepted with a smile on my face. I never smoked anything in my life. Inhaled the smoke and began to cough something vicious. He laughed and patted my back. He looked at me and said slow down mama, have you ever smoked before? Managed to say no through my gasp for air. He laughed at me and said, well I'm Paul what's your name pretty lady, who don't know how to smoke? "It's Linsey" I said blushing.

Feeling silly for just smoking whatever this handsome stranger had. Hell, it could have been crack for all I knew. He looked at me and laughed. You never smoked weed before little momma? I loved his slang. No one in my life acted at all like him. My dad had his moments but even he was prude and stuck up. Smiling I said no and figured I better call in to work. I started laughing suddenly. Can I have some more I said with a smile? He handed the blunt to me. By the time, the blunt was gone you would have thought we were best friends. Saw him ignore a few calls as we talked, and I made a joke about him being well liked but I thought nothing if it. He asked where I was parked, and I offered him to take a ride. He opened my car door, and I heard a female voice yell, "PAUL! Paul! What the hell? Yo, are you leaving?" He looked at me quickly and said I'll be right back. You stay right here. I smiled and I stayed my ass right there. As he walked away, I realized that my new boo might not be bi-racial at all. He had flavor and he had a little bad boy in him. A normal woman would have headed for the hills on his ass, but I was in deep. At this very moment I should have seen small red flags, but I was already seeing our future in my head.

He was light skinned with a bronze glow to his skin. He had a brush cut and dressed like a thug. I didn't care at all. I didn't see color or gender. I saw his vibe. Whatever he was I liked It, and he would most diffidently be mine. He wasn't black or any gang affiliation, but he wasn't playing a role either. He just was who he was. Like me in a way. I never fit in a box with a bow like all the other white girls and I'm guessing neither did he. He got back in the car, and I asked, "what was all that about? "Nothing he said lying, just a woman who works for me was a little upset the way we left things after our meeting. Nothing you need to worry your beautiful head over. So, tell me about you he said. What's a lady like you doing in this area of town? I was dropping off a package I said. He looked at me with a glare, "to who?" "You a drug dealer he said laughing." No, but I knew some I thought trying to push any thoughts of that out of my head. I wanted to be nothing like my dad. He lived two lives and kept my mother in the dark about it all. Leaving me to pretend I had no clue of the women coming in and out of his office. Or the party's he was involved in. My poor mother would die thinking her husband was a saint, but no one could bare to hurt her in that way. Tell her the truth about her dirt bag of a husband. My mother had never even seen another man naked or been touched by anyone but my father. So, we let her live in her own fairy tale. Paul was staring at me now. Yes, I said, did I miss something? No just admiring you and how your so calm. I laughed out loud and said I'm high as hell. He laughed, I never ever smoked anything I said. I just wanted some attention from you. Is that right? Yes, I said with a smirk on my face. He got closer to me and pecked my lips. I was in love with this man's vibes from the very beginning. I have never been attracted to a white man or any man that was not chocolate skin colored. But there was something about this man that I just could not let go.

My father was calling me now and I knew I had to answer. Hello daddy, I said with annoyance. I just wanted to be left alone. I did what I said I would do so back off I thought in my mind. Did you drop off the package he asked? Yes, I did, and it all went to plan dad. I got to go. "Ok! but be here early to greet the new account manager. He has a lot of clients he is bringing with him and that's going to increase our revenue stream. I'm not sure you understand what our company is about to accomplish. He is a good guy too. No more of your thug choices. I turned down the volume on my phone so Paul wouldn't hear anything else. Dad, who I date is my personal business. You have your life and I have mine. I knew that would shut him up. He wouldn't dare challenge me. The hoes he messes with were trash. He snuck them out the back of the office every chance he got. Even sick he managed one or two every now and again. You, ok? Paul asked. Yes, I said trying to cover the phone so my dad wouldn't hear his voice in the background. I will be there with bells on Dad, but I'm not going to pretend to like anyone for any reason.

I knew my dad was fuming but I didn't care. I was the

one holding our company together. I made all the risky looking delivery's and met with all the future investors, if that's what you want to call them. I was going to live for me for a change.

Paul was so sexy, and he knew he had me too. He grabbed my face and sucked my bottom lip. Just met this man and already he had me open like church doors on Sunday morning. He was already Sucking my bottom lip. How in the world could I act like a classy lady now if he was sucking my face on our first meeting? Wait I said, I really like you and because of that I want to slow things down. He looked at me and smiled with a devilish smile. What if I don't want to stop and I want you now and always? I looked at him knowing he was just talking but I wanted to believe every part of it. I want to meet up again. I said pulling away from his embrace. Ok he said what days are you free? I will just come by and get you.

I laughed because I was a busy woman and there was no just coming to get me. Here is my card, I said handing him my business card slowly and holding his fingers longingly. Call me when you can arrange a nice sit-down meal. When you can devote your time to me and me alone. He looked down at my business card and then into my eyes. "I like that" and then he got out. "Bye sexy lady." he said smiling, showing all his pearly whites. I sped off happy as hell. Not knowing he would be my demise years to come. I was so shook for his love. Even if I had known he would be my undoing I still would have given him a chance.

We became inseparable from that week on. After

about a year of messing around he decided he wanted to marry me. He had shown how devoted he was to me and had never hurt a hair on my head. I gratefully said yes. He cut off his former life for me. Paul was prince charming with long package to go with it. I had no complaints at all in the entire year we were together, and I was anxious to start my life with him. We moved in together and got engaged to be married. Life was turning around for me. I was happy to get up every morning to my new life and that was a welcomed change.

. When we picked out our first home together, I remember we made love on the kitchen counters and the relator walked in on us. We met at the house both of us excited. He walked up with a lit blunt and I with my favorite wine and two flutes. We both chuckled at our celebration tactics. He passed the blunt and I gratefully received it and handed him a glass of wine. As I walked around the house, we noticed the back yards pool. I knew we had to have it. There was fountain in the middle and a waterfall separating the different depths. I started to undress, and he laughed but followed my lead. He cupped my ass and pulled me closer. I could feel him slightly biting at my neck as I walked further into the water completely naked at this point. I bent over and grabbed my toes exposing every inch of my sweet goodness. He slid his fingers down my dripping cookie. My clit got so hard and throbbing with his touch. I got on my knees in the water on the stairway. The water jets were spaying my inner thighs. Paul was behind me now. I Could feel him opening my pussy so he could slide inside. I felt his hard dick pressing inside me. I was so wet for him, I needed him all the way inside me. He thrusted inside me and grabbed my waist. I screamed out in pleasure. He pounded in and out, my pussy was throbbing now. I felt like it would explode. He picked me up onto the side of the pool and began to suck my clit in and out of his mouth. He inserted two fingers inside and slowly went in and out. I was in pure ecstasy. I lifted his head and slid into the water. I kneeled in front of him putting his long thick dick in my mouth. Stuffed as much as I could before I gaged on it. I swallowed that dick while rubbing his balls slowly. I felt his balls get tight, so I stopped just to tease him. I got up and ran to see if the balcony doors were open. I slid one open and walked into a beautiful kitchen. Marble flooring, glass transparent stove. Titanium appliances. This was everything I had asked for. My father oversaw helping Paul find a house, but this was so lavish and not at all what I expected. I was so happy right now I could float away. I hopped onto of the countertop and put my bare pussy on the counter in a split. Breakfast daddy! I yelled playfully. He came running in and turned me over and buried his face in my booty. I could feel his tongue fucking my pussy as he slid his finger in and out of my booty. I would be scared to admit it, but I liked that shit. My pussy was dripping, and he thrashed his long dick hard inside me. I could feel the pressure building up and he was pumping faster and faster. Slapping my ass, I felt tingles down my spine. This was what I've always wanted. Nice house, excellent job, and a handsome man to have children with and share his view of the world. Paul was into it now. I could see his face get serious with love making. He turned me over and looked deep into my eyes. He slid deep inside me and began to grind in circles so close I could feel his balls on my pussy. He was sucking my lips and kissing my neck. In any second, I would explode with pure ecstasy. EXCUSE ME! I heard the realtor yell, and the people with her gasp for air. We looked at them shocked and completely indulged in our sex games. We want the house I said. I sent in my bid already I lied. So why are you here? They looked at us stunned and hustled outside. Paul looked at me and laughed. He kissed me and said, I want you to be mine forever. And I will be I said in complete bliss.

Chapter one

Lexy

College was all politics and appearances. Hell, I was only there for the men and extracurricular activities. I had no clue on my major and I needed my loans and financial aid to stay afloat. School for me was my getaway. I hated going home or being home.

My mom was not trying to be my mother but my best friend, slash maid and errand girl. If she needed cigarettes or liquor, I had to make the run. She did not care how I viewed her, and she never has. She even had me pick up a bag of weed on my way home from school sometimes. She had a car and was able to get around simply fine. So why ask your kid to get your drugs? If my mom wasn't drunk or high, she was mean as hell. I felt bad to see her intoxicated, but it was better at home if she was. She just left me alone which was better than following me yelling and screaming. I just wanted a mother who acted her age and respected our roles in each other's life. She wore my clothes and shoes. She got her hair like mine and went to some of the same hang out spots I frequented with my friends. I tried to purposely not see her. She was hip, and my friends didn't mind but I did. It was weird looking across the dance floor at the crowd forming, and it's your mom twerking in skimpy shorts and heels. She wore colorful lace front wigs and eyelashes to match. She looked good but not like a mother good. She always looked like a video vixen on her way to a photo shoot. She made sure she was at every party or club that was popping. No matter what I had going on or if I needed her. I wanted to see something to look up too, maybe a professional I could become one day. I even wanted the discipline and rules. I couldn't blame her completely for how things turned out. she had been hurt and scarred. This started when my dad was shot in a shootout at a party my mother was having for him. My dad received a raise at work, and we were going to celebrate.

I was only seven years old at the time and I can barely remember his face now. I think back on the night the police officer came to get me and let the sitter go home. The way my babysitter looked at me with tears in her eyes, I knew it was something horrible. This one bad moment spiraled our lives out of control. His death hurt my mother deep. She stayed in her room and my aunt took care of me for most of my life. At one point they started fighting over my care and she kicked my aunt out of my grandma's house. I never saw her or my cousins until I graduated high school. My mother cut off her friends and family. She went through a depression that seem to never end. My dad was my mother's light, and when he died, I think she died too. There are moments I see her smile but it's often looking out into space and I'm sure it's a memory of my father. She blames herself for what happened to him, and she can't let it go or forgive herself. Before my father's death my mom was a church going woman.

She was home all-day cooking and being a mother. She sold Avon in her spare time and paparazzi jewelry. She was happy and content with her life and found ways to build us up as a family every chance she got. She never left the house without makeup or her hair being exactly right. Now, she is just out here willing out and it wasn't a phase. It's been this way for years. I feel my mother is gone and this bitter woman was left in her place. She made sure I knew who's house I was in and who I had to respect or else. I was a live-in house cleaner and verbal punching bag. I know we had it rough but there was never any food or toiletries in the house. I wanted to help but she made it so hard to be around and coexist. The days of me feeling sorry for her was over. I was done. I was making my move and getting out of this place finally.

I was in college now, I made it captain of the cheer and drill team. No one could or can tell me nothing. I had big plans that would change my life as I know it. Nothing was going to cause me to stay in the same lane I been in. I was going to be known for more than just a small-town girl with a shitty family. A team of my choosing and I was going to make the best entertainment company Canada has ever seen. We didn't have to much night life, so my plan was perfect. I just needed to get my girls and some guys to be on my team and down to work hard. I already knew how thirsty they were to get out on their own and earn their money. So, it was about who could keep their mouths shut and be loyal to the cause.

I saw a chic named Jessica and I knew she was ready and open to my ideas. She was a hoe and didn't mind people knowing or gossiping about it. I kept my distance only because she was so live. I like to be low key with my slick shit. But now was the time to reach out and see if she was down. I went to cheer practice and sat right by her while we stretched. As soon as I sat by her, she looked up, "what's up Lex?" "You never sit with me so just be upfront with it." I laughed and smiled. "Is it a problem with me sitting by you?" "I'm not trying to cause any problems, I joked." She smiled. "Nobody likes me she said, always got some stuff to say about my life and what I do." "Not me" I said trying to sound innocent. It was true though; I never had a bad word to say about her. I just listened to gossip or laughed as it was told to me. I never repeated it unless you tried to cross me, and nobody was that stupid. I played for tears, and I always got them too. "So, I'll get straight to the point jess, I need a few trustworthy people to go on this money journey with me. I'm putting together a team to make an entertainment company to take over all of Canada. Are in?" I could see in her eyes she was scared shitless. I knew it was a no. so, I just smiled and started to get up. "Lex." "Yes" I said with a little annoyance in my tone. "I'll let you know" she said sounding as if she was really something special. "I don't need to tell you to not speak a word of my

business to anyone right?"
"I'd hate to have to open
my mouth about you boo."
And I got up and blew the
whistle to start practice. I
knew she was going to be
back, but I wanted her as
my first recruit right hand
man but nope she fucked
up. I was on to the next
one.

  I needed a real ass rider,
and she wasn't it. I could
see the pussy assness in

her eyes and face. During the routine I decided to kick it up a notch and see who could really work it. I told everyone to do a 30 sec freestyle and I would let them know if they made the extra video opportunities. It was a ratchet shit show. They were competing against each other and twerking all on each other. yes, these tiny boppers were ready. I laughed and said I'd get back with them on the girls

I select. Just as I thought Jessica was hitting my Facebook. Asking if I could send her more information on the money opportunity, and did she need to audition too? I was laughing to myself hell yes bitch! You got to audition, shouldn't took your ass so long to ask more and decide. But that chic is and was fine. Sexy even to me and I don't even go that way. I was most diffidently going to get her ass but didn't want her to know. I wasn't going to make it easy I'm just a bitch that way. So, I'd leave her ass hanging until tomorrow when I posted the girls I wanted to be I my promo video. I wanted at least four girls to dance and flip around to a nice beat with no words. Smiling and blowing kisses to all the horn dogs in Canada without getting our asses beat by our parents. I didn't care really. My parents were shitty and didn't care at all what I was doing or involved in as long as I didn't bring the police or any other enforcement officers.

Chapter two

Got home maybe thirty minutes after I ended practice and I could see someone sitting on my porch. Jessica didn't waste any time, did she? I knew it was a chic her ponytail was flopping around. Jessica had come by my house; she was so eager to learn more about the opportunity I was throwing around. I approached with a smirk on my face, I sucked my lollipop slow and looked up. "I hit you on the book" she said. "I know, I was going to hit you back" I said with a nonchalant tone. "So, what's up jess? You didn't come this way to sit on my porch, did you?" "I want to be in your video" she said. "You know I got what it takes. I see you watching me. That's why you came straight to me. I'm no hoe and I'm not trying to look like one to everyone no more." You a hoe if you are loving on multiple men and women. You are a stupid hoe if you are doing it and not making anything from it not advancing. I said, at least if you going to be a hoe or look like one you could be a paid one. I'm not saying that's you; I'm just expressing my point. We on the field working our asses off for free every day and weekend. We could be doing the same things but making bank for it. I love to dance and perform but I hate staying at my parent's place. Ya dig? She smiled "same here. I stay at my uncles now that my mom is in jail again. I need to leave there asap I feel him looking at me and watching me closer by the day. I

don't want to be the girl
raped or on the run I need
some bread I'm almost 22
now you can live with me
she said." Feeling a little
happy inside I couldn't help
it. I low key admired her, I
always had. She did what
she wanted when she
wanted, and until now I
always thought she didn't
care what anyone thought.
The thought of us living
alone together made me
giddy with excitement. Ok,
Here's the deal I said. I'm

looking to make a video for online purposes only. And only to those who need to see what we are working with. I'll make us a page online and we make up routines just like we do for games and charge people for the entertainment. Keep in mind these are horn dogs, so we need to jazz it up some to keep their attention. But we can only include the loyal ones we can trust. We were all over eighteen so it's legal to pay for our services. Most girls had their own lives, but some lived at home still. This whole thing is on a hush hush and tomorrow we will see who ran they mouth about it.

"LEXY!!! LEX! WHERE THE FUCK YOU PUT MY DRANK! ILL BEAT YO STUPID ASS YOU DON'T BRING ME MY DRANK!" "Shit!" my mom is up; you feel like walking some? "Yeah," she said and pulled out a perfectly rolled blunt. "They say I got opium fingers; I make them look fresh out the wrapper." She smiled and passed the blunt. I inhaled hard, trying to wash away all traces of my home life away. Whatever I could do to be out of the house I would. I was positive jess felt the same way. From this point on we were partners, and we won't stop till we meet our goals. Failing wasn't an option. I was making everyone fair game to grab as a client.

Nothing but money on my mind and from the desperate look on Jessica face I knew she felt the same fucking way.

We walked up on a man washing his car. He looked to be about maybe thirty-nine or forty. Handsome and in decent shape. He smiled big and ushered us over. Hey, are you of age? I'm not trying go to jail for messing with a minor.

"Yes," we replied in unison. Wanting to laugh, but keeping it cool I smiled as sexy as I could, praying nothing young and silly wasn't showing. Well, I got a party I'm throwing for my guys, and we would love some pretty ladies. I smiled and he handed me business card. "Think on it and call me or txt me anytime. There will be a ton of money for you ladies and maybe something we can do every weekend if you are good." I'll let you know I said, and we walked off.

   After that long but very refreshing walk in the neighborhood, my mind was calm, and I had a promising idea on what part she would play. Jessica's conversation and cool demeanor changed my whole mood and thoughts on her. I had found my partner.

Chapter three

Jessica

I really like Lex, but something just didn't feel right. I can't pass up on a potential money opportunity either, not while my mom was still locked up. Uncle Pete was nice and all, but I can't deal with his ass no more. The sly looks and sexual innuendos I wanted to run away but I knew I could not just go on the run with nowhere to stay. I was almost 23 and I could be out, I just needed the money to make it all happen.

Not sure about Lexy yet. She seemed like she had an ulterior motive, or she just was out for self. I did not know, but what I did know was that she was a hustler and about her money. I needed that in my life and after last night, I had to be on my way out. He walked up behind me, grabbed my waist and said, "one day you're going to see I was a good man and stubbled off with his drunk ass. Like I wasn't his flesh and blood. We were family! How gross and disgusting. Why would my mother even bring me here? At that moment I knew I had to start making moves to get my own place. When my mom dropped me off here, she said "make sure I lock my room at night and the bathroom at all times." Now I knew what she meant. He didn't have woman of his own and wouldn't get his act together to get one. He wanted me to cook and clean and wash his clothes. All the duties like I was his wife. I didn't cook at my house. I did my homework practiced cheer. I couldn't even get my homework done here let alone practice my cheers. He would wake me up before school to wash his dishes from the drunken snacks he had while I was asleep. He was so serious about me doing my part be he didn't even keep up with the maintenance on his house. I'm not at all bougie but I like clean and consistent hot water. The washer and dryer up and running, so I can have fresh clothes. The trash taken out to the curb every week at least. If I didn't clean and cook the house would be a pig sty and he would have Liquor for dinner. The next day I went to see my mom at Walworth penitentiary. I had to see if there was anyone else, I could stay with. I didn't know them but hell, they had to better than my uncle. Grandma, aunt, something.

Last time I saw my mom was a few months back. When I saw her, she looked like a different person. Before she went into prison, she was on drugs. Stripping to pay bills and support her habits. I was second best, and my older sister was out of control. I didn't know where she was now. I blamed my mom for her hardships and her disappearance. When she should have been there for us, she was out with a different man every day. Even though it was her job and she needed to help us, I couldn't burden her with my shit. I wanted her to get better and stay better. I'm going to figure this out on my own. Guess me and Lex are going to become closer than I anticipated because

I'm done waiting. Moving up the ladder.

Chapter four

Paul

It must have been fait seeing those little chic's walking today. I just spoke to my boys about finding some virgins for the pussy party, and boom there they were ripe for the picking. Washing my car and turned around and they were walking by laughing and doing cheers across the street. The little bitches were turning me on just talking to me. So young, so tender, and sweet. I wanted to be the one to deflower them if they hadn't had sex yet. Or just hear them being deflowered by another man would get me off. Had a thing for fresh young pussy. It was amazing I had not been caught up yet. I was a pimp of sorts in my past and I was itching to get back in the game. I just needed to find some fresh young faces not scared to take risk and be down for the cause. I needed loyal girls ready to listen and take charge when needed. But all that was jumping the gun I still had to get Linda to agree with it. My wife didn't have an open mind when it came to side hustle. She liked women but she wasn't down with hoes around me all day without her knowledge or approval. But all I needed right now was my pussy party to be jumping. I had promised about fifty people I would provide entertainment and fresh young pussy. It was up to them to have the bands to get it. I had them pay five hundred upfront to get the location of the party. I had no choice but to make it happen. I needed this party to thump, or I was five grand in the hole. I couldn't have people looking for me. I Think I'll head to The House of Sin and secure some strippers. I had to get the dancers set up, maybe even snatch one of the DJ's and a trapper to have drugs on deck. Always need that at the party, but the most important thing was the virgins and females. We had a bet going. Out of three or four virgins at the party, someone had to nail them. If you got more than one or had a threesome, we all had to put in three hundred extra and the money was yours. Not to mention the live sex show in the back room. Charging $500 cash app only paid at the door. In return you get a goody bag full of handy trinkets that can be used during the evening and that includes the show but not front row. VIP was $1500.00 and was front row seats, with your own private dancers. Fruit and champagne were also in the suit too, alongside the vegetable tray. This was a secret invite only affair and it would jump just like I planned. I just needed to make a few calls.

"Hey, John you trying to go see some pussy at the spot tonight?" "Got a proposition for you." I had to call john and get my boy involved. He has always been down with me. Even when I was nothing living with my moms in the hood. John came through and kicked it so I showed love whenever

I could. I used to be the biggest promoter in the city and john was my right-hand man. I brought all the celebrities here and hosted the maddest parties that were invite only. I met Lindsey and my life changed. I wanted a family and to be in a stable situation for once, but I wasn't sure I would get it if I didn't jump on the chance with linsey. Her dad had a great company and a lot of money to pass down to my kids. I left and never thought I'd look back. But after my fortieth birthday I felt useless. kids were leaving for school soon and I needed room to do me and live my life the way I wanted. I was cramped and stuck in my own mind. So, I was going to start living again and making my own money my own way. Lindsey was no longer holding my leash.

"John you there?" Yeah, he said, I'm down to go see

some coochie and have a beer with an old friend. Must be good if you're calling me. Yeah, I said. We stand to make fortune if we play our cards right. "Ok he said," "I'll see you there at say ten?" Ok cool I said trying to sound current and not my age, like I wasn't old trying to hide my wrinkles with tanning cream. Age was nothing but a number. My only problem was getting my wife to go along with new life and attitude. She had never seen this side of me, but she would learn today. I was going to get sexy and urban. I'm not wearing the suits I normally swag into the club. I can't walk in looking like a mark, a walking lick. Not to mention my boy would clown me if I came looking crazy. I walked in the house probably looking like I was up to no good. As soon as she saw me, she scrunched her face up turning all red in the cheeks. "What's going on babe? I already know somethings up by that dumb expression on your face. You been acting crazy the past two weeks if we are being open and honest." She said almost yelling by the end of her statement. "I can't keep acting like things are ok with us if they are not. Is there something you want to tell me? Maybe vent.?" I looked at her for a minute feeling almost sorry for her. She didn't deserve this. She had always been there for me and deserved an explanation for the changes I was about to make in my life. I didn't want to lose her, but I knew if I told her what I was about to do I most definitely would lose her and all we built over all these years. "Look baby, "I said with pleading eyes. I just need to get back to being me babe. I need to find myself again while still being a part of this family. Nothing is going on, I'm fine. I'm just reaching out to some old friends and catching up. Need to be able to express myself outside of my family and wife. Is that such a crime? Can I not have both? "She looked at me with pure hatred in her eyes. I knew I wanted her I just wasn't sure I had the will power any more to keep her. I still look back at the first time I saw her. So young and tender, she was so sweet, and I loved her the moment we met eyes. I changed my universe for her.

Chapter 5

Linsey

I already knew I had a problem with him when I married him. Love was blind, and I was blinded and blind folded. He had me wrapped around his fingers. I would do anything to see him smile and to get that good dick. All my friends warned me that he was trouble. "He will always be him Lin." My bestie would say in annoyance. "One day he will go back to his old ways." I did want to ever believe her but now I was seeing how right my bestie was. See, I had Paul's phone bugged. Everything that he received, I received too. You have to love sprint services. He had no clue that for five years now I have been checking up on him. He ran off with a stripper in Vegas and he thinks I don't know. Punk ass boy, please. There was no working man convention in Vegas. He played me like a fool. The girls' name was Rockey and she was his main bitch back in the day. Why he liked ratchet hoes I would never know. I was so far from that world he once lived in. and I know he still fantasized about. I was not going to lose Paul to the streets or better yet, not to a hoe either. I was done letting life take what was mine. If Paul wants to play these games, I could play too. Why he thinks he can throw a party with the biggest club and all the high rollers invited and not tell me is ridiculous. Did he think me a fool in real life? I was going to give him ample time to come clean and be truthful. I'm going to ask to be his partner and if responds in the negative there will be so much hell to pay. I won't be made a clown to all the people in my city. I too have a reputation to uphold and a past he is so oblivious too. My family may be prim and proper, cut from a perfect cloth but I was not. I always did my own thing to secure the bag for my family. I allowed my family to think the business was thriving and that all my dad's arduous work paid off. I was the puppet master in all things concerning me and he was not about to ruin what I built, and dam sure wasn't going to be around town with some hoes, I didn't know or give permission too. He was mine! I had made this man into something from nothing. Who the fuck does he think he is?

Chapter 6

Milton jay

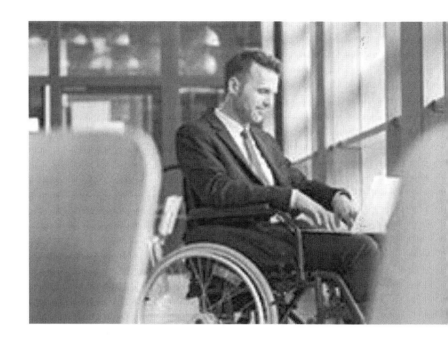

Good morning sir, is there anything I can do for you? Yes! I said with a tone of I'm better than your stupid ass. Like duh bitch, I want the same coffee I get every fucking day. Why not have the shit ready? I never understood this girl, but she was smart and quiet. She didn't ask many questions and ignored any illegal activity she may have seen. Help like that was hard to come by. Shanice had been my assistant for five years now. ever since my last assistant went missing. Yes, I offed his ass. The nigga transferred ten cents to an account every time I spent a dime, like I wouldn't notice 100,000 missing from my savings. Account manager alerted me right away. I gave him two chances to tell me, and it still didn't sink in that he better fess up. Chauncey had been my ace for a minute and despite so many people telling me he was a snake, I continued fucking with him. I couldn't leave him on stuck after all we been through, and his kids depended on him. He wasn't a snake, he was just out for self-preservation. But the money in an account was the last straw. He could have just asked for money. But after that I decided to hire only females. More loyal, and they know not bite the hand that feeds them. After he went missing, I decided to still send 3000 monthly to his wife and kids. It's the Least I can do after I sent his ass on down the river.

Shanice was different, she didn't care what happened if that check came every two weeks. The hush hush bonuses were her favorite part of the job. Not to mention when anyone from my family comes into my home or office, she plays the role as my caretaker. I am sure I was going to hell for this lie, among other sins too but My daughter and family believed I had multiple sclerosis and needed constant care. I didn't want things to be this way but when I asked my daughter Linsey to take on the company and keep laundering the money she refused. This kind of job is passed down to the children. there was no out. I took on more than I could handle by smuggling drugs into my factory for 306 mafia. But the money was good, and I needed to keep my factory open to keep the money laundering going. And if I let that stop, we were all dead. My daughter, her kids, me, and anyone I loved. That was a defining fact. So, I had to do what I had to do. this ridiculous charade was doing the trick for now and it was a significant risk to change things up.

I never wanted to get back in this and I most diffidently didn't want this for my baby girl. It's complicated and I'm not sure if I made the right choice or not. It all started at the two. A Small little hole in the wall but it was the spot. All the people that were anybody would at least show their face in the club once a weekend. I was there with my boys, and I was so thirsty. I wanted that bag so bad I could smell it. I was sick of my grandma's basement and the looks when I pulled up in my little hooptie. My plan was to make all that change that night. I saw the owners of the spot about to start up the poker game in the back. I ran up and offered to do anything I could to help and just be around. He looked me up and down, sizing me and my boys up. "Yeah" he said with a smile. Bring yaw dumb asses on. Let's see just how down you are. We walked in and sat down on the extra folding chairs in the back as they all took their place at the table. The air was already thick with weed smoke and the smell of brandy. One by one they told us who they were and what part the played in the 306mafia gang. "So, what you think? Yaw still trying to hang? Aint no question on if you are down once you in. Boom! The door swung open, and a group of naked women came rushing in. Clearly faded but dressed like they were going to prom. They straddled each of them and gave them an all-access pass to all the goodies.

They looked at us and said, "If yaw was down with the gang, theses be your bitches too. These are the 306 hoes and he slapped one on the ass. We love them though." They all said with pure joy in their eyes. I could tell the ladies do anything for them. I could not lie I was Impressed. Not by the women, but by the power one possessed by being 306 Mafia. In one night, I could change my whole life and reputation. My mind was everywhere from the crime to the money and what the hell I would tell my grandma. I didn't get to decide if this was the choice because the events that played out next put me in the mafia immediately or signed my death note.

Boom! My ears started ringing and my vision wasn't clear. I saw smoke and body parts all over. Was this real life right now? My boy was bloody on the floor next to me. I jumped up and grabbed a gun next to me. Big p grabbed my arm and pulled me to my feet. Three police officers busted through the door and dro picked up an Ak-47 and let them have it. Their bodies jerked every which away and blood painted the walls a red so dark it was almost brown and seemed to give the smoke a red eerie glow. Big P yelled let's go and we grabbed everyone that we saw scrambling around or breathing. Jumped in the van and sped to get help and see who was missing. "You in this shit now bra!" Dro yelled in my face as he wiped his bloody face off on his shirt. Where in fuck are my hoes yelled Big P! I sent Lola and Nicole in the other car with that new nigga and Jaffar. Miami was bleeding out in my hand in the back seat. She was so pretty I couldn't help but think about the events that led her to this moment. I watched the life leave her eyes and her body went limp. I nudged Dro and he looked back. I shook my head and looked down at shorty. I saw the tears swell up in his eyes, but he pushed them back. Dro was the right-hand man to the OG of the 306mafia. They were not allowed to show emotion, it was a sign of weakness. But at this moment with so much blood and fallen soldiers I don't think anyone would judge. At this point he was being a boss for his own sanity hell I was too. I wasn't ready for this life but apparently it was ready for me.

We pulled up to an abandoned building and the gates swung open and the vans drove in. Three white men came running out ready to help. but to me anyone needing the help was already too far gone but can't hurt to try. We got everyone in the place as fast as we could. It was a hood horror flick. People in beds everywhere bleeding and moaning. I couldn't watch anymore. I looked over at all the sadness and I saw the pure rage in Dro's face. I got up and grabbed his arm and said "let's go find out who sent the pigs to the club. This whole thing was a set up. In my mind the enemy would want to see what happened and who got shot. We drove by the backroads around the club and sure enough the BMF crew was right there scoping. All I could see was that beautiful girl dying in my arms. No more than 18 years old. Guilty by association. Now these hoe ass niggas were guilty. "Jackpot!" Dro yelled with glee. I pulled out my new gun and blasted with hate in my heart for the men who did this and all connected. It was at that moment I realized fate had made the choice for me and had chosen correctly because the feeling was pure bliss. Lighting them fools up like that was a release of pressure. Dro was blasting, my boy freeze was blasting. The sound of the metal meeting metal. The smell of gun powder and fresh air. It's like time stops and all you see is the moment you're in. I loved every minute, and I wasn't scared. I ran up to the car and made sure they were dead, and I saw the life leave just as that chic did in my lap earlier. I looked back and saw all the niggas staring at me, Dro ran up and pulled me to the van. It was quiet and I noticed people looking at me. "What" I yelled? "Your covered in blood bra! You went fucking men in black on us and left the van during a fucking drive by! Wtf?" I looked down at myself and saw the blood. I looked crazy as fuck. Good

I thought if I was going to be a thug, I wanted respect. I looked my boy sin in the eyes and shot him right in the face. "Shut the fuck up!" Dro and freeze hopped in the van, and I sat up front with Dro. I was mafia now and I couldn't lie it felt invigorating. I was nervous about the future and letting go of all that was good in my life for a new one

Lex

I was done waiting around. After me and jess got cool, I knew I can get out here. We are meeting Paul tomorrow and I need at least 3 more girls to make my crew for the party he was planning. I was already in everybody's ear about picking my girls based on who picked up on the new routines. Out of all the girls me and jess would decide who would be coming to the party. Today was the day and I'm excited. I was going to stop by Paul's house on the way to school. He said I could and ii knew his wife and kids were gone. I just wanted to talk but if things went further.... O well I thought. I wanted out of the life I was living and in to the one I dream of. No more waking up to my mom's cussing me out drunk or fucking strangers on the couch for me to see. I didn't have family day or dinners waiting at night. I was done playing nice when everyone was mean and soulless. As soon as I walked up to his house, I could see him outside smoking on the balcony. Must have been some good stuff. I could smell it from here. I called him and he answered with a smile on his face. "Meet me at the shed in the back" he said. Snuck my little hot ass to the back shed, and I already had my own blunt smoking in the air by the time he showed up. "Look at your sexy ass" he said swinging me around to his chest to face him. He was so handsome. Something about him was dangerous but so soft at the same time. I grabbed him, close as if I knew what I was doing. He said "wait, is this your first time. No, I lied with the straightest face I could muster. I needed this to work, and I needed the title as queen b with the girls and him. I wasn't trying to be wifey so fuck his wife. I slid down my dress and let it hit the soft rug under our feet. He pushed me back onto the futon rough, but it tuned me on. He licked my hard nipples and sent chills down my spine. I couldn't believe this was happening. So many times, before I dreamed of this moment and how perfect it should be. I wanted to be the one to take control and spring myself upon the man. I was taking control of my own life finally. I was enjoying this in its entirety. He kissed and sucked my neck while cuffing my breast. He began to get lower and lower with his kisses' "God!" I screamed as he sucked my clit. I began to grind my hips into his face not giving two fucks if he could breathe. I could hear him tearing away at his belt and jeans. I'm coming I yelled! Don't stop baby please! He dug so deep inside my pussy I swear I was being fucked. I came all over his face and was eating me up. He looked up at me and stood up. Paul groped his long erect dick. What you going to do with this little mama? I leaned forward and tried to swallow that dick. I sucked and bobbed my head going to the rhythm of my pulsating pussy. He grabbed my head and pulled me up and kissed me so passionately as if I was his one and only love. I felt so loved and wanted. He thrusted his long hard dick inside me. It took my breath away. I gasped with each stroke. I was moaning in pain, but it quickly turned to pleasure. I started to scream out. I wrapped my legs around him and started grinding back my pussy was about to explode. I thought I was going to pee the pressure was so strong and then I came so hard my legs shook and my toes curled so hard I had a cramp. Paul began to grab my booty and my waist pounding harder and faster inside me. This all my pussy! You hear me? He fell hard on my chest, and we laid there for at least an hour. We smoked a blunt and he offered to give me a ride to get some food and somehow on the way I'd get near my school and go in so I wouldn't miss my all my classes. no one would show up to my house from the school and get me killed literally. I was known to miss class for my mother's bullshit and today it was my bullshit so couldn't let my mom find out. Not until I had a place of my own and a car to get me around. That was all doable and this nigga laying on my booty was about to make it possible.

Jessica

Where the hell was Lex? I know she was coming to school we were texting this morning. With the extra stuff we were getting into I needed to make sure she was good. Plus, I was too excited about today's cheer practice. I was praying we had at least two girls that would be down to get this money but if not, on God I'll be out there with Lex making that bread. It was not an option at this point.

My uncle had come in my room that night asking, "did I want to drink or smoke?" I looked at him as if he was crazy. He said, "come on girl lighten up you almost twenty-three now. Right?" Better to know what's up at home then get lost out here in the streets. I was shaking to my core. The way he was sweating, already half drunk. His shirt was stained with food and what smelled like beer or piss. He leaned closer to me, and I saw him groping his self. I jumped up and yelled you my fucking uncle! He looked at me and said I'm not your real uncle fool. He walked out my room slamming the door laughing loud like I just told a joke. I looked around my room to find something to wedge against the door. I refused to wake up and see his fat ass sweating on top of me. I didn't get much sleep that night. Kept listening for the door. Woke up feeling like I ran a marathon. Couldn't do many more nights like this.

I had to find a man who could help me get up and change my life. This shit was dead and when I got my money up. I was literally out of that bitch. I hated times like this. I was stuck in my own demons. I wanted to reach out to someone just to vent or even listen to their problems. Once I was up, I was up, I would never allow myself to feel this low. I jumped up to grab my things for school

I was calling Lex ass fuck it. "Hello," she said, and I could tell she was already high. Where the hell are you boo? You still coming to school, right? "Of course, baby we have some much-needed business to get done. My high ass is on the way right now. I had to seal the deal or two she joked, I needed to make sure our train would flow easier." She said laughing uncontrollably. I was lost but I knew she would disclose information later. Ok I said with a relief in my voice. I could calm down now that I knew she was on her way, and we were still on to find our girls for the meeting tomorrow. This was the only thing going for me right now and I couldn't mess this up. I wouldn't allow Lex to mess it up either. I hadn't known her long, but she was impatient and would let her ego get in the way of what is important and that's eating together, helping each other, and keeping true to ourselves.

Lex

Dam I had so much fun riding and chilling with this old ass dude. But I could not lose my cool or give away that this was all new for me. I was a boss and I needed him to see I could handle the girls for the party and all future parties to come. I was going to show him that I was the only one who could. I needed to have back up when the girls tested me. I needed him to let them know I was in charge, period.

We were getting in the area of my school, and I didn't have much I could say to explain why I would just get out the car on the corner. I didn't want him knowing my school, address, or family members. I had to keep this secret life a secret, and that means my real life a secret from the shady shit I was doing behind closed doors. I looked over at him, he was so relaxed, and he drove like he owned the road and all the cars on it. I think I was just dickmatized and I had to get my shit together. This man was married and only wanted sex and money from me, so I need to do the same, right?

Ok, I had fun I said, you can drop me off over here. What? He said with a confused face. Live over this way I said, and I don't want to be seen coming in. He gave me a look that said I was full of shit, but he pulled over and politely dropped me off. Waited for him to pull off and then I made a short cut to get to the school. I made it before Lunch hall closed. Fixed my clothes, put on some lipstick, and sprayed a few sprays of my favorite spray. "Love spell." Ready and stupid excited to see who was going to be working the party with us. More importantly I needed to show up to this meeting and impress them. I was praying that the three I was thinking would show out wouldn't let me down.

Jessica

I was so happy to see Lexy sexy ass come walking on campus and in school. she was the only reason I came here today. She was something else entirely. But I was really starting to like her. She was Ying and I was yang. I can't lie I was happier these weeks we been hanging out. We were up to no good, but it was all for a cause. I was leaving my old life behind by any means necessary. I refuse fall victim to my uncle or any other fool because my mom couldn't provide me a life anymore. I was grown now. I could take care of myself. This was just helping me get there faster and I would most defiantly get a real job too. I wasn't going to get lost in the game.

It was the end of the day when I saw Lex again, she was trying to get all the girls to go outside on the track so we could make a private announcement. All eyes were on me and looking back my way. I could see the looks and I knew it was because I was Lexy's right hand chic now. They trying to see if I'm going to help lead this announcement, but not at all. I was going to play the wall and come in just like everyone else. I did not want them to think I got any favors. I'm just me Bish. I practiced my parts until I was dancing in my sleep. I can't lie, Lexy was not playing around. we practiced until she was tired and dancing in her sleep too. The other girls got the text about the extra practice same as I did. I got the text and made plans to attend. I was better now, and it was not because Lexy liked me better.

We lined up and started our stretching. I could hear all the voices talking about who they knew would make the extra event. I was cracking up in my mind. "Get in position" lex yelled and we all jumped in place and watched her give us the end and beginning cheer for us to follow. Lex made any dance or movement look so easy. I just hoped I looked half as good, and I would be happy. I danced my heart out and I know every girl there did too. I dropped and shook my little curves as hard as I could. When the song was over, I was excited because

I knew I killed that routine, and everyone else knew it too. I was eager to see the end results and tell Lexy how I felt. I know I should tell them myself but that wasn't me. I wasn't at all scared to step up to the other girls I just liked my life to be low key. I don't want people knowing I have any say so about anything. When I get out in the light, I tend to attract the wrong kind of attention and almost always get myself in some nonsense. I heard music start again and the girls looked confused. I was ready and gave a look like come on let's go to the other girls.

I could see Lexy about to blow the whistle. She caught a glance of me in the back and gave me a look like really? I looked away and prepared for the music to start. I started grinding my hips, dropped to the floor and did a slow split. Popping and bouncing up and down to the beat. I was so fire I could feel people looking at me. I didn't care I was looking good and loving the attention. For the first time in my life, I was confident in myself. I looked up and Lexy was looking at me. We met eyes and I can't explain the vibes that passed but she pulled me to the very front and gave me a look and the rest of the squad like, try me! I looked next to me, and I could see the green in their eyes. I was not going to let Lexy down. I didn't want to let myself down, I knew I was one of the best and today was my time to shine. This routine was all about being sexy and that was my thing. I started grinding my hips and hit every move just as I should. I looked over to see that only four other girls were dancing with us. Lexy looked and blew the whistle. What's up she said? Most of their eyes looked down and then someone spoke up, "We don't want to look like strippers!" she said with the most serious face she could muster. "Ok!" Lexy said, "That's cool. I had a special event I wanted us to be a part of, but I can see it's something I'll have to have special invite only. Don't think that later I'll be letting yaw in because the ship has sailed. Practice is over!" She said with a tone that no one wanted to stand up too. The girls just grabbed their bags and stomped off. She looked at me and the other girls that stayed and counted us off to start the routine. As soon as the music started, I could tell the girls wanted the same thing we wanted. That bread. It was clear as day the kind of event she was planning.

The only thing I was worried about was the

other three chic's trying to take what me and Lexy were trying to do. We started this together and decided we would always tell each other what's up and keep our shit straight. Me and her against the world. None of these little hoes were going to steal my shine. It's not that I was a hater, I just know how people are. They see an opportunity to get ahead, and they would jump at it. I heard the little bitch whispering between songs. Saying she ready to get down if needed and shake her ass for cash Cuz that's what our performance looking like. I know that's what we wanted but I was thinking we would get girls we could teach and lead. I did not want to bring anyone in that I would have to be in competition with. Lexy was more confident than I was, and I could see she wasn't worried at all about shit. She was more confident and readier than I have ever seen her. She had plans to take over this city and I can now see she was taking no L's. We practiced and came up with three sexy ass pyramids where we were spread eagle. Twerking and shaking till we were sweating, and I wasn't for messing up my 30-inch-long curls, but for the right crowd I may let these curls fall.

We were looking beyond ready for tonight and I

planned on making all of them fools fall in love at first sight of this ass and titties. I had my hair done and nails polished. I took my uncles wallet and went to town. I even got me and Lexy matching fits. I can't wait to see they eyes when I whip out those sexy ass channel sheer one pieces. Long strapped thong in the back pulling sexy over my shoulders. I love how it makes my ass look so fat and plump. I was not going in this game half Assing nothing. I know I shouldn't be so concerned with Lexy and how she looks but I had a special place for her already. She only one who saw anything in me. In these months we been friends she has helped me so much. I was so stuck in my own mind about what people thought of me and my personal situation. She never judged me, she listened and held my hand as we both vented out our life's frustrations. We held each other close and cried about life's bullshit. I have never felt so close to someone based on just our struggles and how we are going to overcome it together. I had her and I know she had me, period.

Paul

Dam that little pussy had some power, but I was scared I had deflowered her for sure. She was so tight I could feel every breath she took tightening on my dick. The slightest touch was driving her wild. She was amazed with me. She was looking up at me like I was a God, her God. She made me feel so good, just being around her and showing her things. I had to boss up though. For all I knew the little girl does this to everyone. That's what I wanted right? I know I'm married, and I didn't plan on leaving or anything. I was just having fun. But dam if I couldn't get her off my mind. That smile and the gap in her teeth. It's like she knew what to say at every moment even if she had no idea what to say at all her sexy ass would still save face somehow.

I had to get focused and get these girls to this meeting to be checked off tonight. I was praying Lexy could really dance as well as she could fuck. The way she looked in my eyes and held me so close I had a feeling she had my back. That scared me because if Linsey found out I was fucking her, little Lexy may get hurt, not to mention what may happen with me. But I couldn't think about that I had to get my ass to this meeting. First, I had to round up the girls and make sure they weren't going to show up in no bullshit. Stupid kiddy plastic earrings and jewelry. Some bright colored Walmart bra and panties or just dresses.

I wasn't sure but I would not let these little hoes mess up my reputation. Not to mention the risk I was taking period by getting back in the game, my wife would kill me. Part of me just wants to tell her, but I know she would be ready to flip. Currently, I wasn't asking permission. I was just going to do me regardless of her wishes. So why ask or explain at all?

I told Linsey I had a meeting with the football league. I was an assistant coach, so I used this excuse any time I needed an out.

I pulled out my phone and dialed, I could see her face in my mind. Those hips and thighs were stupid, and her legs were thick too. How in the hell is that possible in a size seven? Her thongs were a fucking small. "Hello," she said sounding calm and collected. She

Was not feeling the same as I was, I was frantic. This meeting must go as planned. What are you doing, I said, trying to sound like I was serious? I hope you getting your girls together and going to put on a show. I'm real serious about my work. I could hear her breath in hard. "I'm ready Paul. I got them here now practicing. I'm serious about my work as well. Is something wrong? Why you all up tight? That dick needs to drain, right?" I could hear the humor in her voice. I couldn't help but smile. Lexy. please be early like spoke on and be on point. Yes, Daddy she said with a sexy tone. It took me right back to her lips around the tip of my dick. I could take a double dose of that right now. My manhood started to rise just thinking about her skin and lips. Wasn't even sure if I could smash her again because I had to get Shawty out of my head before I lose my shit. But right now, I must focus on getting my party to jump. After our conversation I was confident they would be early so I could see what they put together before I showed my mans. Not thinking I sat my phone on the top of the refrigerator as I grabbed a coke and hopped in the whip. I remembered it right as I pulled out the driveway. I walked back in the garage and wifey sitting right there going through my phone. With a face that spoke a thousand words. I was frozen watching her scroll through the messages or pictures I didn't know, but I knew I was sure as hell about to find out. She was so hot, she was shaking. I could see the rage in her squinted eyes. I didn't dare say anything or try to take the phone for fear she would really loose it. Linsey was a quiet but deadly type of chic. Don't let the heels and blazer fool you. She was a bad ass white chic with a serous mean side. "How could you.?" She screamed with tear swelling up in her eyes. I have always taken care of you! I cooked for you she screamed, while hurling a coke she had been drinking. It splattered all over my white button up and fresh foams. Fuck! but I didn't move or try to duck because I knew I deserved it. All of what she would do I deserved every bit. "After long hours at work I still come home and cook." "I still come home and clean up after you and those grown ass kids. What life do I even have outside of you and my fucking father?" I refuse to let you do this! I won't be a made a fool of she screamed and pulled out a slender, pink, and gold-plated pistol. What the fuck I yelled and threw myself to the ground. I crawled to the door and managed to get out. I ran to my car without looking back. I sped off with her pointing the sexiest gun id ever seen at my back. I had turned her crazy I thought, but where the hell did, she get a gun from and why? I couldn't stop seeing her with tears in her eyes. I hurt her and for no reason other than my selfishness and ego. Sadly, I cared but not enough to stop. I had no choice now. I had to get this party to pop because a ton of wild people have money invested and I dam sure couldn't tell her that. It was just best I let things die down and let my little shorty know to watch her back and not to answer any calls from wifey.

I sped down the boulevard as fast as I could I was already late to meet the girls. I walked up to the location, and I hear men talking and laughing. I expected the worst but the girls must have done an excellent job. Hell, I did not know my mind was so racked with what the hell my wife was doing and would continue to do. "Daddy!" I heard Lexy scream, she came bouncing out in the sexiest leotard I have ever seen. Her ass looked so good I almost forgot to warn her about the danger I put her in. I looked over and all the boys were smiling giving me thumbs up and saying how excited they were to be doing this with me. I knew it was just because I came through for them, but I couldn't help but feel accomplished. My whole life was now on the line all I have is this looking up for me right now, and Lexy fine ass. I knew there was a chance she was with me for seniority over the situation but that was a chance I was willing to take I needed something to take this pain of a fleeting life away. Same old shit and that was now changing. I just feel so bad for hurting my wife.

LEXY

Come on yaw, get in the truck. "Dam where the fuck you get this shit from?" My girl said with a tone. I didn't have time to even discuss all the details with her. O boy went ghost and I wasn't about to mess up our opportunity because he flaked. I have the address and names. we are going with or without this nigga. She looked at me and yelled for the other to get in.

I can't lie her attitude was so bomb. I loved how she just went with the fucking program and now she was taking charge. It's like I built a monster, just like me. I was loving every bit of it. I was smiling so big, I felt on top of the world. I knew I was going to kill it. My girl had the outfits from head to toe for us and I managed to trick this fool into giving me a car to drive. All was right in the world. I won't lie letting him touch on my body and do coke off my stomach was horrid, but this ride was worth it. Right? I could see Jess looking at me. She was trying to see how I felt for real. She understood me like that. We didn't have much family and our mothers were concerned with personal highs than our lives or just couldn't be around. We had each other's backs since the day we connected after practice. I know I need to tell her the truth about me and Paul, but I think it may ruin things, and I liked out affair being a secret. It wasn't hurting her. So why do I need to tell anyone anything?

We pulled up to the building and I saw three cars outside. I started to get tingles and butterflies in my stomach. I looked at my crew and saw the fear in their faces yaw, we got this. We just keep it hot like talked about. Make sure your facial expressions are sexy and make sure your personal dance is an expression of how you would or want to fuck.

Everyone laughed and I took out my box from the trunk. I passed around a goodie bag for each girl. Lip gloss, perfume, wipes and two shots with a small glass bottle of Pepsi. Omg they screamed. But jess was quiet. I had her bag personalized and had matching jewelry in our bags. She looked at me like I had never seen anyone look at me. We walked in confident and ready to take over the world. I knew I had done too much for my boo, but she deserved it.

As soon as we walked in, we might as well have been on stage. The men were lined up hands in their pockets or passing blunts that looked like cigars. The air was chunky with weed smoke and cigarettes. Seeing that we are being watched and graded off our entrance alone. I told my squad to line up and do our sexy walk inside. Once we were in the middle, I asked one guy with a full head of dreads and hands full of bottles if he could play our music. He quickly dropped what he was doing to assist us, but I could see he got an OK from the fat guy in the corner before he helped. I would make sure to please that one by some personal attention. We were going to get continuous money not just one-night money. The music bumped and we did our thang. I walked over the boss in the middle of our routine still staying in the dance and bent down in front of him shaking my butt as hard as I could, I looked back at his face and smiled. He was in heaven, and I loved the feeling it gave me. Right as I got out of boss man's lap, I see Paul come busting in. He looked at me with surprise like we were not going to be here and couldn't work without his being there. I shot him a lustful look and got back in our show. I could see by his face he was worried about something but right now I had to conquer, I had no time to be thinking about him. This was business.

John

I have to give It to my mans. I don't know where he found these girls, but they were exceptional. Hell, I was excited, and I was working the party. When we sent the promo out with the girls on the front of it was a wrap, our phones were blowing up. I can't wait to get started on the décor and the poles we were going to rent. The party was on, and we were jumping again. Our names were already out in the street. I was sitting with the crew taking orders and selling tickets when a blocked number keeps calling me back-to-back, I hate blocked numbers. It's starting to get suspicious, and I just decided to answer fuck it.

I don't want any trouble, my name is Lin, I wanted some information on my husband. Please don't say you don't know because I'm beyond powerful and you sir are not untouchable. Ok, I said trying to sound calm. All I know is he is working with a few new chic's for this party we trying to pull off. I'm not in the loop to nothing else. "Where is his ass right now?" She said with a shriek of anger I could feel deep Inside even though she was yelling through a phone. I knew she wasn't playing, a woman scorned was liable to do anything out of revenge. I wasn't trying to be a part of her war path. Ok I said, we just left a job, and I don't know where he went or is going. He left when I did, and I can't get him on the line I lied. I was sending a txt to him as we were speaking to warn him. "Nice try" she said coldly, and she hung up. I got a txt back and I knew it was probably Paul, so I rushed to the phone thinking man I'm so glad you responded, but it was her, his wife. I told you not to play with me, so I'll send you and Paul a little message by lighting you up. I looked around eerily and went to the window slowly. My boys looked at me and took the safety off their pieces. I cannot believe this was a suburban homemaker, that had us outraged like this. "O shit"! my boy yelled, I looked outside to see my car was a blaze. I ran to the door and bust it open thinking, I would at least see the bitch. But as soon as I opened that door I felt hot led in my legs. I fell to my knees screaming in pain. I could not believe I had been shot and my car blown up because Paul could not leave the bitches alone. Before I could crawl to the door to call the police I was put in a car and bag over my head. I could hear the fire and my crew fighting back but the car I was in never slowed down. God, please let me survive this and I will never put on another party again. I will never take another girls virginity if I can get out of this alive. I never saw how bad my ways were until I was almost dead. Would I get killed for this?

Linsey

What was I going to do with is fool? I was aware he lied but now that I was looking at the video, I felt bad. But the life my father had forced on me was not one you could just follow your heart. Not if you want to live. All I knew was my father was in business with some serious people. I tried

to decline working with them when my father took ill. I was carted away in a bag and my son threated, and he was two hours away at boarding school. I always had no choice but to launder the money through the company and that meant staying on top and being the main CEO. I now saw why my father's actions whereas such all these years.

"Yo! what the fuck you want me to do with this old

man? "My radio went off loudly reminding me I had to decide dumb dumbs fate. Beat him up and drop him off at the hospital. I said as non-challan as ordering a number one at McDonalds, and it was done. My next stop was to see what that little bitch had going on really with my husband and did she think she was running away with him. I had to stop at cheeses cake factory for a slice of pie and a drink. I needed to calm myself before I killed this young naive bitch. I planned to give her a chance just how I gave john. Just one chance.

Lexy

When we were done, I went to the dressing room and freshened up. We talked and laughed about how good we all did and who got the sluttiest out of the group. I just sat back and laughed. I enjoyed every minute of this. I had worked hard, we all did. We deserved this. We heard a knock at the door. I walked over and said "yes?" with the cockiest tone I could muster. I opened the door and they walked in with weed and champagne. A slender man with a suit jacket and jeans on handed us all flutes. This was about to be a night to remember I could already tell by the glow on everyone's faces. We were already on ten from the shots and the high of being on stage. This was the best feeling, and nothing was going to stop my shine. What is your name, I said as we all put our glasses in the air. You can call me smiles, he said with a big Chester cat smile. His teeth were perfect and when he smiled, he was so handsome. His eyes made you forget your troubles for that moment. I looked at him and laughed. Ok smiles I said, pass the blunt this way. Jessica came to my side and we both gave each other that look. He was dumb fine. Small as he was, he looked and acted like he could and would pick my thick ass up and toss me around. I had to stop. I literally just got out a nigga lap. I don't think Jessica could help it either. We both laughed nervously and sat on the couch together. We puffed the blunt and the other girls started playing music. Jess looked at me and I looked at her. I am feeling nice right now she chuckled the words out. You are looking really nice too I said. It got quiet and awkward for a second. I was not sure if the vibes I had been picking up on were right? I'm sorry I said, feeling stupid and out of place suddenly. I got up and she pulled me back down and groped my breast in a way I had never felt before. I immediately felt a tingle down my spine. I turned and she met my lips with hers. In our minds it was just her and I. Should I be doing this I thought? But any thoughts of doubt were soon washed away with the champagne I had her drinking off my body and the shots me and smiles took off hers. I looked at jess and I said let's get out of here. WE grabbed our jackets and noticed all the other girls had gone home,

Jess laughed and said we are the chosen ones. I laughed and pushed the button to start the whip. We hopped in and I look to see all kinds of texts and missed calls. I got calls from a blocked number and a message from Paul's phone that I knew right away was not him. Hey, where are you? I need some of you again. it said, and I always came to him. He never asks that, nor would I tell him. I knew something was up. I listened to the messages and Paul's wife knew about us for sure. She is demanding I speak to her face to face like I was a complete fool. I thought about maybe lunch tomorrow but after I heard the urgency in her voice, I decided not to meet with her at all and let Paul handle his own personal problems. Hell, maybe I should have left his ass alone. I can't lie I was scared a little bit. I'm not the one to be fighting. I also did not want anyone to know I fucked him.

I must have been looking like I saw a ghost because jess grabbed me asking if I was ok. I just looked at her and said, Let's stay out. Let's get a room for a few days, while we have the party. a day to chill after if we can swing it. She smiled and said OK cool let's stop and get clothes. The way that message sounded and the text I was not trying to even go by my house, but I knew I needed clothes. I had to suck it up and get my things. I could not let this bitch get me scared to go home. I dropped jess off and told her id be back in 20 min. I hit the corner and decided to take the back roads to get to my house. I pulled up and parked in the alley just in case someone was watching my house. checking to see if my truck pulled up. I came in the house quiet, making sure I did not wake my mom. I was not asking her to do anything. I grabbed a bag and put a weeks' worth of clothes and jewelry in it as fast as I could. I already had my work gear in my car, I just needed my cosmetic bag, and I was out. Something told me to take my mommas burner just in case Linsey was crazy for real. I texted jess I was about to leave when I turned to see my mom standing in the doorway.

"Where the fuck you think you going? You sure as hell didn't ask me to go. I guess you grown now?" No ma, I said as nice as I could because I knew she would slap me silly. And I could not come to that party tomorrow looking a mess. "I talked to Paul's wife she said. With a sly look. I know you messing around with her husband, or she wouldn't have come looking and asking questions. I looked up, Huh? "Yeah, play dumb if you want but she going to whoop your ass. Leave her property alone! Do you hear me?" Yes mam, I said, and I meant it. I did not want this kind of drama at all. I gave my mom a hug and ran out the back door. I could hear her yelling my name, but I was done. I had to pick up Jessica. As I was leaving the alley, I saw a black SUV parked in the front of my house. I drove out slow trying to not be seen turning the block, but it sped up. I picked up speed almost sure it was that crazy white woman. I looked over and saw the SUV speeding up to the side of my car. I almost ran off the road I was so scared until I saw Paul's face. He was urging me to pull over. I pulled over and he got in my passenger. Where have you been, he said? I know you not fucking none of my boys. I can tell you been drinking too. Paul! Why the fuck is your wife talking to my fucking mother ?! you can start by clearing up this messy ass shit! He looked at me with a look of shame. "Yeah, she found my phone and saw all the pics I took." What pics? I asked with a surprised look. O hell you are so dumb I said with an evil look pouring out of me. Tell that bitch to stay away from me. This is not my issue. He looked up and said, "yeah but she may have lost it." She ran me out the crib with a pistol. Lay low for a bit or at least until I can make thigs right with her.

Ok, well for that I need my pussy ate good, I said softly and smiling. For all this trouble I need to orgasm down your throat. He slid down to the floor of my car, and I pushed my seat back as far as I could. He lifted my skirt and slipped my panties to the side.

He sucked my pussy lips until they were throbbing. I could feel a pulse in my clit and I grinded my hips into his Face. I could feel his wide, hot tongue inside my pussy. Ugh I moaned with pleasure. Faster I said as I fucked his face. I was about to cum. Eat this cum I screamed and squirted all over his face kicking my legs on the roof of my truck. Thank you I said with a sexy ass grin on my face. I grabbed wipes out my bag and looked at him one last time between my legs. O I'm going to need some spending money too I said with a sly look on my face. I need a hotel and food for the day's I'll be hiding out. I can't get beat up before the party tomorrow night. He handed me a wad of cash all wrapped in a rubber band. I was on I thought, who cares if a bitch was after me. I had money, a new truck and I was about to go explore this new freak escapade I was on with Jessica. This new life I was taking on was paying off and I wasn't about to stop now.

Jessica

I walked in and I could smell the nasty smell of throw up and cigarettes.

I hated this house. I'm thankful I'm not on the streets but dam.

Jess! I heard my uncle say. "That's you?" I could hear him cackling drunk and then coughing up a lung. He was standing in the hall in a dingy wife beater. no pants just white underwear and long black socks. He looked homeless at home. I could smell him from here. "Where the hell you been looking like that?" he said staggering towards me. I moved out of the way and didn't answer. Hey uncle, I said getting past him and into my room. I just knew any second Lex would show up honking and ready to go. I closed the door and locked it. Throwing all I needed in my bags. I didn't care if I ever came back here. I knew it was only a matter of time before something happens, and I kill this son of a bitch. I heard the doorknob twisting back and forth. "Wakey wakey eggs and Bakey, he said laughing. Why you are locking doors

in this house!" He yelled
now, sounding insane.
"Open this door with your
fine ass!" I hated when he
laughed, it sounded
ominous. "You grown up
now, fuck it. I'm not trying
to be waiting no more!" He
started beating and
banging at the door now
and I was scared he would
get it open. I grabbed all I
could out of my room and
slid out the window. I
looked at my phone hoping
lex was nearby. I sat on the

corner for what felt like forever just thinking. Praying my sister and mother were ok and deciding I was not ever coming back here or to anyone else's home. I was done playing nice. I waited over an hour and still no lex and she didn't answer her phone either. I called my girl jazz to come get me before my uncle happed to look outside and make my night any worse. Jazz pulled and I got in with a smile like everything was cool like I always did. She didn't ask why I had my life in my bags, or if I was ready for tomorrow. She just yelled roll up Bish! I know you got some weed, and I got white owls. She was exactly what I needed right now. We rode up to her crib and we sat in the car for a bit. I got a call from a random number, hello? I said trying to sound proper and intelligent. "Hey girl its Paul." Who? I said suspect. "Yō boss." O I'm sorry how can I help you? "I wanted to know if we can hook up really quick. Ask you a few questions and maybe grab some food." Ok I said. I needed a guaranteed spot in the game and he can provide that. I needed everything from a home to soap to clean my ass. Can you come get me now? Yeah, he said. I'm on James and 28th. Jazz looked annoyed but I didn't care I told her I was going to secure a bag and she was cool with that. We smoked until he pulled up. He was in a black SUV with tinted windows. I gave jazz a hug and hoped out. I got in and I could see he was Litty. Hey, what up ma? You ready for tomorrow? Lexy got yaw asses looking good. Yeah, lex is the shit with the dance shit. I said and i meant every bit of it, but right now was about me. So, what's up I asked? What's got me on your mind? "Them thighs and titties he said laughing. No, I'm playing you seem cool. I wanted to get to know you and make sure your mental was right for tomorrow." I'm ready to get this money I said. I got a lot of needs I plan on getting it. I put my hand on his leg when I said it. He looked at me with lust in his eyes. You a virgin? No, I said smiling. Let me show you? He opened his fly and let me take control. I pulled his item out slowly still holding his balls when I sucked him in my mouth. He tasted salty as fuck, but it wasn't smelly, so I kept going. Truth be told I loved a working man the thought of him working for me and then fucking me turned me on. He started fucking my mouth, so I knew I had him. The way he thrust so hard in and out I could feel and taste him in the back of my throat. Feeling the control I held drove me crazy. I sucked and pulled his balls. Feeling his muscles and legs shake, I pulled him out my mouth and straddled him. I slowly put him inside me. Ooooo, I could feel his dick pulsing inside me as I rode him as fast and as hard as I could until he was grabbing my booty begging me to stop. Kissing me all over my neck. I came twice on that big dick. I gripped his balls as I was coming. I even bit him on his arm. For his age he sure as fuck surprised me on how swagged he was. He knew just how to hit it and where to grab me. He pulled out some wipes that I knew were not his. In fact, I want to say they were Lexy's but I know if she was shagging this dick, she would have told me. Plus, she told me she was a virgin. My girl not gone lie to me about no dick. I would share a dick before I fight or lie on one and that law. I texted Lexy to see if we were still on for tonight. I knew I was wrong for fucking Paul, but I needed to make sure I was good from now on.

Paul, I said as low and sweet as I could. I need some money baby. I live with my uncle, and he just tried some bs if you get my drift. I can't go back there. He looked at me sadly and handed me a wad of money with a rubber band on it. I smiled and kissed him on the cheek. He grabbed my chin and stuck his tongue down my throat. I was wet again,

and I had no time to act up again, so I pulled away and hopped out his truck. Thanks, I said with a naughty grin on my face. Now where the hell was Lex.

Lexy

I know I was wrong for leaving jess hanging for an hour or so but shit I had to say bye to the best dick I ever had. I at least had to get my pussy ate and grab some food. Hell, I had him get us a room at the hotel deco so I figured she would forgive me. I didn't tell jess about me and Paul, I didn't want her thinking nothing and now I was stuck on him. After we got the room, we fucked again. I just knew his dick was made for this pussy. We were fucking raw and all. He even said his wife and him would separate. So, in my mind what was I doing wrong? I texted Paul a sexy pic of me and called Jessica. She answered on the first ring. Dang she said, I laughed and asked when we were linking. Come swoop she said. I got some good weed. Me too I thought, and I can't wait to get faded. Paul said I could kill the mini bar too. We were about to turn up. Where you at? Red lobster at the bar she said. How you at the bar I asked? Just come on she said. I got up and hopped in the whip. I was still on cloud nine, but I had to focus on tomorrow night there is no love once I get inside the party, and I had nails and hair to do. I pulled up to red lobster and called jess. Come on girl I hate sea food I'm not feeling it. I got one rolled and it's about to be lit and smoking so bring your ass. She came stumbling and laughing to the car. What the fuck bitch. I got out and helped her inside. What you eat? You need some grease and caffeine or something. I don't like sea food! I'm allergic to shellfish. I took three allergy pills! She yelled slow and sluggishly. "Then why come to eat here?" She looked at me and spoke really slow. My new boo wanted to eat here so I just went with it. I started cracking the fuck up. I had to pull over. Shut up bitch. Don't do that anymore. I said through laughter and tears. I drove us to Timeout, and we got our usual. Best chicken in the O and my favorite cheeseburger and fries. I hit the blunt and noticed me and jess had the same weed. She knotted her bag up and I let my mind go with the smoke that drifted out the car. We pulled up to the hotel and I saw Jessica's face. O shit bitch you got some big bread if we are staying here. Yeah, I got a boo too. We gave each other high five and ushered over a bell hop and parking valet. We were on the way up and there was no going down.

Paul

I had to go home some time so why not go now? I pulled up to the house and saw linsey's car out front. I walked in with caution. I knew she was angry and on a war path. Something I had never seen in her. She was sitting on the couch in the great room just looking at our family portrait. Lin, I'm sorry baby I said sounding as sad as I could. I truly was sorry. I didn't want to ever hurt her. She was the women I married and always wanted to be with. She looked at me and asked did I know where my boy john was, I said No with a weird tone. Why does he matter and what did she know about john? How did she know john existed.? She had a sinister look on her face, and I could hear muffled screams and bumps from my office. What the hell is that, Lin? I left some of your new work issues in your office. I walked slowly to the back and peered in my office. It was a bloody mess. I saw his panicked eyes and from the cuts and wholes in his body I didn't think he would make it. What the fuck have you done Lin! What did he ever do to you? O come on Paul, I thought you would be thanking me. He wasn't loyal to you. I even put plastic on the floor and walls to protect your manly décor from being ruined. After your betrayal I thought you would be thankful I still cared. She was truly scaring me now. Lin, you have killed this man! "No fool! she shouted and threw all the papers off the table onto the floor. "He will be ok. I just beat him up some. I was going to do this to you but then I didn't want to see the scars when

I was riding your dick." I looked at her with disgust on my face. How could something so beautiful so delicate do something so malevolent? This was not the woman I fell in love with. I have been seeing her outburst, but I never thought her capable of this. "Lin, let me take him to a doctor. He needs help before he is dead in my office. What was your plan? Why are you doing this?" I said through my teeth, trying to contain my emotions and anger. "I wasn't going to hurt him, but he is a liar. if he was going to lie, why did he give me any information? He was weak, like your restraint." She said coldly. Her lips flat like a board and the corners so tight they were wrinkled. Ok! I'm taking him to a doctor. I will say I found him like this. "You will talk to me and tell me the truth before you take him anywhere."

She was standing in front of me now holding a pistol. See, I'm done letting men take advantage of me. I looked at her with a puzzled face. "Thanks to my father and side hoe bitch! I took on the company and laundered money for the lowest kinds of people. I risked my life and was raped, trying to keep my ass from going to jail. I have had to work for fear that my family would be slaughtered." She sat down, Putting her face in her hands. The gun was now on the table, but I couldn't take the chance to get it. I didn't want to fight her at all. I never knew her pain but looking back everything makes sense. The late nights, and secret phone calls. The worry and stress like work would come eat her. I tried to hold her, but she pushed me away. No! she said. Get your hands off me! I can't stand the thought of you touching me after you had those whores all over you. I did so much to make the men in my life happy. But I'm done. Little bitches always getting in a man's head." I'm going to tell you a little story that happened to me today. Right before I came in the garage and saw all the pictures and text from all your hoes, I went by my father's house to cook for him and care for him. I was going to give his nurse a break for the afternoon. I didn't want my car getting wet in the sprinklers, so I drove around back and parked by the back patio. I walked up to the door and saw my father and his nurse fucking in the den. She was dressed in red fishnets, and he was pouring oil all over her. Candles lit and music playing. There was wine and strawberries with chocolate. I was stunned. My father was incapable of caring for himself and was not mentally able to consent or be involved in a sex act. It had been three years since id had a normal conversation with him because of his so-called condition. I just sat there and watched them fuck. She was some actor. She sat there and acted like this man was old and near death. But why asked I? why do this to someone you love? For personal gain! She looked at me with hate and hurt in her eyes. There is no love or loyalty in the game of life and the pursuit of your own happiness. I got up quickly, I reached out for her arm. hoping to touch her. Maybe I could show her I was still down for her despite my actions.

She picked up the gun, guessing I would go for it and struck me over the head. I fell back, seeing nothing but darkness. I could feel her dragging me. Lin, Lin please I pleaded. The lights were getting brighter. I could smell the ink and paper and I knew I was in the office too. I'm not sorry, she whispered in my ear and kicked me in the head.

Linsey

I wanted to forgive my husband, but I couldn't. I knew he was not going to stop seeing the women. He had been with three women this week. I knew he was fucking raw too because the dumb little slutty girls were asking if he was clean. One of them named Jessica said she may need a plan b. I had his phone and couldn't believe the non-sense he was spitting.

What was so sad is, he would act like he was so in love with me. He was giving me new jewelry and going to fuck and suck with another woman. Who could I trust in this life? Even after all I did for my father, he would do this to me. Faking his medical condition? He said he didn't want anyone to know of his condition and now I know why? He was a liar. He only cares for himself and that little bitch he had lien to my face every moment of the day. I wonder if she was even a real nurse. She was in on it, I was positive. But the joke would be on them when I was done. I refuse to continue to be the fool for everyone. My next plan was to move all the money to my private account in Tahiti. I found a beautiful home seven miles off the beach. I would retire in peace. No longer would I be the fixer, mother, sister, lover, or daughter I once was. All the roles were about to change and when I was done everyone would be begging me or running away. That's only if I decide to let them live. I just need to be sure my dad was doing this by his own free will. I could not believe he would do this even with all the proof in face.

When I saw my dad, I was in shock, and I had to be sure he was not being forced into the act. I did not know this deceitful man I was seeing earlier today. No, he was dear old dad as I remembered. Laughing and telling jokes but as my mind recalled the events of earlier today, I knew my dad had been truly foul. I watched as they prepared for my arrival. Putting his braces on his legs. Got the chair by the bed and his little toy nurse even put on the scrubs, as if he needed help using the restroom. I watched as my heart broke. I didn't want to see him. I couldn't bear to see him lie in my face as me and my family were the ones on the line. Life or death for me and my kids.

Milton jay

At first being in this chair was driving me crazy but then I embraced it. It gave me more power. I was able to run everything right from this chair. I begin to see it as a throne of sorts. I had gotten it costumed for comfort and leg rest. It was gold and red my favorite colors. I was going to get it engraved but thought that was dumb in case I ever had to leave it behind at crime. I had my nurse slash girl toy at my disposal. Everyone expected me to be sickly, so I was never questioned, and the work was done well. All my people have been on my payroll for years. All my peeps that dro and I had working now were old heads. Even gangsters had to settle down some time and have kids and wives. The plan was sound and had worked now for years. My daughter was no longer a problem. she has been running the company and getting the money all sent to their owners with no mishaps. I was proud, even if I did have to lie to get her on board. Eventually we would find our way out but until then I'm milking this game for all it has to offer.

I called my nurse into my room to call my daughter before I took off this disguise, but there was no answer. She was missing all day, and this wasn't like her. I did know that husband of hers was fucking up in the streets and she was possibly handling her issues. I wasn't going to worry just yet. I would let her figure it out before I sent in reinforces. I know he was helping some old heads pull together a party and that was all good as long as he doesn't hurt my baby girl.

I had to make a call to Dro to see if he would go to the party Paul was throwing, just to check it out. I may need to have some of that party to be my after party. I haven't participated in a real party in almost four years now. I need to let off some steam. I was tired of my live-in pussy. I wanted a woman that wasn't mine. One I could be whoever I wanted with. I was so tired of this act I had to put on.

In a few years when I have saved enough, I was going to disappear with my family and go to another country. My money would be longer there, I could be free. I just needed a way to tell my baby girl that I had lied to her and paid many others to lie to her. I couldn't leave her here, so something was going to have to give. But for now, I was going to enjoy the lien ass bed I made and lay in it.

Lexy

I'm not sure if it was the roses in my bath water or the water jets flowing all around me, but I was in heaven. I was sipping spiked Kool-Aid and blasting the Ellie Mae station on my echo dot. I had been so wrapped up in the stresses of life I wasn't taking the time out to cherish me. I needed this getaway to unwind and turn up before the party tomorrow. I liked things to go just as planned. I wanted an excuse to get a room and get closer to Jessica. I wasn't sure of the feeling I had or the sensations I got when she touched me. I wanted to see for sure if wanted her or not. I won't lie, she had become my best friend, where I never thought I'd care at all about her. My view of her was so flawed. Everyone's view of her was wrong. I saw her and she saw me.

She came in the room with a drawstring thong and two little pieces of pink cloth covering her nipples. She was always at her best. She slipped out of her sheer robe and joined me in the hot tub. She sat on the far end like she wasn't sucking my nipples last time we kicked it. I could tell something was bothering her. I would figure that out later but right now I was going to enjoy the peace of this hot water. My phone started ringing and so did jess's. I looked at my phone and it was Paul. I looked at jess and she was in her phone too, she peeped me looked away with a sly look on her face. What the hell was that about? Paul wanted to come by at two. I told him I

was with Jess, and he
insisted that I ask if could
still come. I told him no. I
wanted this night to about
us. Tomorrow was going to
be a sausage fest. His ass
could wait. I looked over
and jess was looking at me
with big pretty eyes. She
sat her phone down and
gave me a look like let's go.
I was down and I wanted us
to be friends and secret
lovers forever if possible.
My life had not been so
nice since I brought her in

to my life. We kissed passionately and I could feel both our bodies go limp and I knew, and she did too, that it was real. I didn't really like to kiss until I kissed Jessica. Maybe I was gay. But I loved dick, so I doubt it. Whatever it was I liked it. She laid me flat om the bed and took off my shirt. I lifted hers off her shoulders and pulled her bra above her breast. I pulled her close to me and then there was a banging on the door. Jess smiled at me and said she had a surprise for us. She opened the door and Paul's wife knocked her to the floor. Blood oozed from her head, but she got up. You bitches think you can fuck my man? Linsey looked at Jessica and said yeah, I saw you riding his dick! I have cameras in that truck! Both of you hoes fucking him! He belongs to me she yelled. Until death, you some stupid hoes. But it's all good. You bitches will be the first to Go. At once I knew I had to shoot that bitch because she wasn't planning on leaving us alive. She had big black bags and her boys held plastic. I reached under the bed and grabbed the gun. I fired three shots with my eyes closed. I didn't want to see the blood or the loud noises. I looked up and all three of them were on the floor. I Grabbed out clothes and bags and went out the door. I was dam near dragging Jessica's ass. We walked out the back of the hotel and see a car running with open doors. I reached in and grabbed the bag off the back seat. Jessica yelled lookout and a man grabbed me from the back of my neck. The gun dropped and I knew I had fucked up. I could feel myself losing consciousness, I hit the ground with a ringing sensation that was so loud

I thought I was deaf. I Felt a hot feeling on my back, but I could move my legs and arms, so I jumped up and realized my attacker was dead and I had his blood all over me. I grabbed the bag and started running. Jessica! I yelled. She was stuck frozen just looking at the body. Her eyes were so wide. I snatched the gun out of her hand and put it in the bag I was carrying. She looked at me still standing there.

Come on I yelled, and I slapped her in the face. She looked at me and started running. Thank God I yelled what the fuck is wrong with you we both said. We hopped in my truck and exhaled. I started the engine and we sped off.

Jessica

What in the hell was in that bag Lex was carrying and almost got killed over? Where was Paul, and did he know about all of this? I had a head injury and I had killed a man. I needed answers. I asked Lexi to pull over so we could talk. She pulled into a car wash and washed the car. She sparked a blunt and pulled out the duffle bag from the back seat. I knew it she yelled. It was full of money and jewelry. Social security cards and birth certificates for three people. She was digging in the bag like a wild animal. She pulled out some papers and she begin to laugh hysterically. It's a house she said with a big smile. We are rich with an estate on an island. With brand new identities. Plane ticket that's for two days from now. I was happy and I wanted to jump for joy too, but my sister was still out there, missing. I needed her before I could leave."

What's wrong?" Lex said, "you look like a sad puppy. We are looking at more money than we could ever count." I looked at her, I need my sister. She been missing for a while now. I can leave but I need her. "Well, there is another passport and ticket. "I'm not sharing my money or the house. I grabbed the money and found the deed to house." Lexi was looking at me with a serious face. I know I said. As far as I'm concerned, it's all yours. I shouldn't have invited Paul behind your back. It was quiet in the car. I knew she was mad. "Why were you talking to Paul she asked? After all that's happened tonight, I'm just going to say it. I had sex with him. He called me and asked if he could pick me up. I knew I should say no but I needed to get out of that house with my uncle, Lex? I did it out of security and desperation. Why are you so upset? I know I should have told you but dam. "Because I was fucking him too. Ok! I been having sex with him for a while jess. I didn't think he was so foul as to fuck my girlfriend too." Girlfriend? I asked quietly. "Yes! what you think we doing? I never felt this way about a female. I'm not saying you have answer to me but dam. You start having sex with our boss you should tell me at least. Did you use protection?" No, I said feeling like a fool. "Neither did I. "We some fools I said loudly. "Did he nut in you

Lex asked with annoyance in her voice. I think so I said. Did he nut in you? She said. I couldn't say anything we were both stupid and played by an old fool whose wife just tried to kill us. I can't focus on this right now I said. I need to find my sister. We must get out of town fast. Or we can just be our old selves and go back to school like nothing happened. Lex! Are you crazy? We just killed some men. We need to get out of here. Who do we even have here to stay for? As soon as I find my sister we are out.

Paul

I woke up to find that my office had been destroyed and I was hog tied and bleeding. I looked over and my friend was gone. I was laying in my office with a dead man. He didn't deserve this, I felt so bad I had brought him into this game. His wife always said id get him into trouble. What was I going to tell Johns family? We had been boys for a long time. We had done our share of dirt so maybe this was we deserved. So many girls over the years that we deflowered and turned out. All we cared about was making money and having fun while we did it. We never stopped to think about the after effect of the parties for the women. Just how much we had made off them.

I wasn't sure how long I had been in here, but my blood was drying on my head so I'm sure I'd been in here some hours. I looked to my safe ad been forced open and all my private contents thrown to the floor. My heart raced and my head begin to pound as if I was going to have an aneurism in my brain. My money and my house in the islands were gone. I had hidden that money to escape with. All my years of illegal work was gone. Hell, I might as well die here. My mind was racing now. I wanted war on my wife and who ever she was working with. There was no way she was doing this alone was there?

I wasn't sure of anything now. I was only sure that my wife had finally cracked under pressure, and I was the blame for that too. I had to get out of here. I needed to warn my girls and stop my wife from stealing all I had.

Wifey Lin

I could feel the hot lead in my chest. The stickiness on my dress sticking to my back. People were running around in the hall, and I could hear sirens in the distance. I had to get out of here. My car was waiting for me in the back right at the door. I slid myself up the wall and out the door.

People were gaping at me and screaming. I was bleeding everywhere. If I could just get to my car, I knew I'd be ok. My car would call my pops and id get stitched up in no time. I threw myself down the stairs and hit the door with a thud. I managed to open the it and I could see my car. I ran to the door and opened it using every ounce of adrenaline I had. I fell in and started to drive. Car! I yelled, call dad. The very person I was after, I needed him now or id die. Funny how tables turn so fast. Hello? "Dad!" I yelled "I need help bad. I'm trying to make it to you. I'm three miles away." My voice was drifting. Stay on the phone baby girl he said panicked. Where are you? What's going on? I'm tracking your car he said. Lou! Roger! Go get my baby now! Someone's coming for you baby. They are on their way. Ok daddy I said trailing off. I saw nothing now but darkness. I had no time to pull off the road or end my call. At least I had shown my husband I was no chick to fuck with. Not ever will you Call me Becky Bitch.

Latoya

I knew I needed to get back to my little sister, but I was having fun living free. No school and no rules. I got drunk and high every day with no consequences. I couldn't lie and say life on the street was perfect, but it beat getting raped by my uncle every day. My mom dropped me off to my uncle every chance she got, and I just couldn't take it anymore. I told my mom before she went to jail that I could not stay there but she just warned us to be mindful while we were there and apologized about having nowhere else for us to go. My little sister did everything she could to protect me, but she was not there every second of the day and she barely could protect herself let alone me. I wasn't good and following someone else's lead either and my sis could be bossy because she wanted me to be more like her. She put her emotion into her studies and still gave mom the respect and benefit of the doubt. I knew her secrets though. She had her outlets; she wasn't a prize pony, but she acted like she was so spectacularly great. The truth was, she was just as loose as I was. We had no one to look up too or to call if we needed advice. We were raising ourselves through trial and error. I tried to put my sister on game, but she was too smart and determined to be positive and focus on school and social relationships. Making her own way in life. Seems sill that I was not the same wave as her now but at the time those things didn't matter to me. If you didn't have a blunt or cash to shop with, I wasn't about it. My home life was sad and unhappy. Anytime I was out it needed to be all about me and having a blast. I wish I could see more of myself, but I didn't and still didn't. I prayed for more hope and faith in myself, but it just didn't come.

TODAY

I got up and decided to get myself together. I had been using drugs with my new boy toy John and we had been holding up in his stash spot. I looked in the mirror and noticed an ugly spot on my face like a scab. My eyes were all sunken in and cold looking. I had meth face and it was no denying I had a drug problem. I didn't want to show up to my sister looking like this, but I feared the worst if I stayed here with My so-called boyfriend. He was supplying my every need for drugs or food, whatever I wanted. I heard John coming to our room. He looked at me and said you look gross Toya. Here, I brought you some stuff to freshen up your look some. Go take a shower and get beautiful for daddy. He handed me a bag full of clothes and silk under wear. There were two beautiful lace front wigs. He even had jewelry and makeup. I was in love with this man right now. Why would he do all this for me? He was just saying how I needed to get out and earn my keep. He was tired of feeding and supporting my habits. But whatever the reason I didn't care. I was looking and feeling like shit, and I was about to look amazing. I smiled at him and lifted my face near his for a kiss. He pulled away and said go get yourself fixed up for daddy, then you can love up on me. I Looked away, I refused to show this fool of a man any of my emotion. I took the bags and walked away. I was no fool. I knew his plan was to dam near pimp me out. My mother was a crack head all my life I was used to seeing her get her fix however she could. When she finally lost all hope of her normalcy, she lost her job at the bank and became a stripper. That was her normal job and it supported us and her habit for a while. She let it take over her mental. It became more important than me and my sister. She depended on my younger sister to be my mother when she was gone. My sister cooked and cleaned every day. She did my hair and picked out our clothes. That became our normal routine. Living without her. My sister was younger, but she always was the wise one. She acted responsible as my mom should have. Mom dropped off money, but we were on our own. So, we learned to survive differently than other kids our age. While they were doing summer camps and reading programs, me and my sister were putting on talent shows for money in the hood. riding with the coolest dope boys to stay fresh and eat good. I was the queen of getting what I wanted, and I could thank my momma for that. I kept a pocket full of money and a man to provide. I just messed up messing around with this fool. I started talking to this older guy named Paul. He lived near my house, and he gave me a ride home in a real bad storm. I was having a real sad day so we talked, and he said I could always reach out to him if I needed too. It was all innocent with him at first, but I kissed him. I was upset and confused on my whole life, and he was there for me. I kissed him and he started kissing me back. We made love in the back of his truck over a dozen times. I knew it was wrong to be with a married man, but I had no one else. No one to hold me at night or cuddle me if I was scared. My dad was nonexistent, and my mom didn't care. After the night my uncle came in my room and raped me, I was beyond hurt. I stayed in my room and skipped school. I refused to speak to anyone. I told my mother, and she did nothing, she literally stared at the wall like I said nothing and wasn't there. I started to walk out her room with tears streaming down my face and she said, "I thought I raised you with the smarts to keep yourself safe and away from something like that. You didn't see the signs girl?" that's the only family we have who cares anything about us." I won't allow him to keep hurting me or my little sister! I said it with a tone I know she understood. She looked at me coldly for a long while. Then she yelled, do you want to be homeless, and hurt? Do you want to be hungry with no bed to sleep on at night? Do you want to be taken away from you're your family, sister? and given to a stranger or an eviler person? She shook me hard and spoke. "Then you better watch your back and shut your mouth! You got caught slipping this time! Lesson learned. And don't go crying to your sister either! You know she weak as hell, she may tell someone and get yaw took away and split up like I said. I'm not getting yaw back either. Those cold words stayed with me forever. I didn't want to keep my sister in a bad spot because of me but I dam sure couldn't stay.

I ran away from her and slammed the door. You hear me she yelled! I could see the hurt in her eyes as she slammed the door. She just didn't have the will or the way to change what had happened. I looked at my sister's room and I looked at my uncle's room. I didn't know what to do next. If I told my sister, she would for sure get us kicked out of here. I knew there were worse things than my uncle. I barged in his room, and I looked at him dead in his face. If you ever lay a finger on my sister, I swear on everything I hold dear I will go to the police and show them the tape of what you did to me last night. His eyes widened. You little bitch. Get your ass out of here! I don't want your sister no how! He drunkenly staggered after me. I grabbed my backpack with what little I did own, and I left and never planned on looking back. My mom never even came out the room to see the commotion or to look for me. I knew it was going to be a cold hard ride at life, but anything was better than there I thought. I walked down the street at least half a mile and decided to call my boy Paul. My older sexy man. I told him I was outside walking toward his house. He said he was already outside; he was mad at his wife and chilling in his truck smoking weed. He saw me and came over to see if I was ok and why I was out walking in my pajamas at midnight. I told him I would gladly tell him about my dramas over a blunt and away from any eyes that could see us. He smiled and asked how I was. I lied and said I was good and deciding what to do. He looked around and we ducked off to the back of his house. It looked like a greenhouse we were in, but I didn't care if I could sit down and smoke. I wanted to chill and get out of the cold. I was glad I called him, and I was happy I could talk to someone other than my thoughts. I had told him everything. I told him all about my uncle and how my mom didn't care. I even told him that I thought she was planning to leave us there with my uncle and id have no chance of making it in that home with him. I could see the anger in Paul's face. He wanted to hurt that man. Paul looked at me and said I never had to go back there again. I looked at him and we kissed. I wanted him so bad inside me. I knew it was wrong to lie to this man about my age. I was a grown woman in my eyes and in his too apparently. He grabbed my waist and pulled me close to him. I want you he said but we can take things slow. I like you LaToya and I want to help you get out of the bind you're in. I got someone you should meet. He rolled a blunt and handed me a blanket. He started a fire in the fire pit and got some water bottles out the mini fridge. This is nice I said looking around. "Yeah, this is my hobby turned hustle. I grow Cannabis for a company in LA. I spend so much time here I had to deck it out." I sipped my water and handed Paul the liter. He lit the blunt and I sat back and exhaled. I felt safer in a greenhouse   with a man I knew wanted to screw than I did my own house. I knew he was a dog but at least he knew how to treat a lady. He leaned over and started kissing my neck. How old are you he asked? I'll be twenty-one this fall I said sucking my bottom lip. "I got someone I want you to meet then. My boy runs a club about forty miles south of here. You could really make some good money." He was looking at me now trying to see how I was feeling about his proposal. I'll see I said. Where would I stay? "He got you. Plenty of girls stay there and work in the evenings. No big deal just please don't be on any bullshit. I knew it was shady business, but I lost my job at the shop, and I couldn't go home anymore. We kissed and did some heavy petting. He gave me an address to the club and sent me on my way in a uber. I told him I had no gear to dance on stage and needed to at least get a lace front for my hair before I went to this club. He handed me a hand full of money and I bounced. I made a few stops at the beauty supply store and my favorite store, Victoria secrets and picked up their limited addition black angel bra and pantie set with the matching fur. I arrived at the club looking like a million bucks and I was ready to dance. But when the man john saw me, he wanted me for his self. He was sexy to be an older gentleman and he was balling so I really didn't mind. We talked and chilled all night drinking and eating fruits off my body and a sexy light skin big girl. who was trying so hard to taste me? I wanted to play but I didn't want him to see just how freaky I was. That would come later if he kept his promises of money and drugs. I wanted loud to smoke and henny in my cup. Not to mention at least two hundred a day for bills and fun. I didn't plan on really dancing here at this club my plan has always been to find me a Zaddy to take care of me. Then I could go back for my sister move out on our own for good. I just needed my sister to hold on a little longer, but my plan got totally slowed down and confused. Somewhere between the drugs, sex, and money making I got sucked up in the game. We went back to my man's johns place and started to turn up in the swimming pool. I was on top of the world in my mind. I felt so good and so wanted. I never felt this way in my life. My mother didn't have a nice word for me. I had no man in my life. I loved the security felt when I was with John. Every man around knew I was John's woman, and I was not to be fucked with. He had about three guys there, we all took shots, and they did lines of coke. Me and my little light bright boo were curious as to what the coke would do to us and make us feel. She was the first to participate. She laid back on the couch saying how good she felt and how she never felt this good. She started touching her body slowly and smiling. I wanted to try it too, but I knew I needed to leave that shit alone. My mom was cracked out. I told john no. I said my mom was strung out and I can't be like her. I had to look out for my sister. They all laughed and said this was coke and not crack. I wasn't falling for it. I set back in my chair and lit my blunt and sipped my drink. No one would peer pressure me into anything.

Me and john went back to his room that was just as lavish as the pool hall. Bear skin rugs and fireplace was looking lovely adjacent his California king waterbed. I was wowed for sure. This was no dope boy living at all. He was a grown man. I could smell the cologne in the air and a light scent of smoke. We sat down and he pulled out his bag of coke. I gave him a look that spoke a thousand words and he said with an innocent look on his face. "This stuff is different; it will relax us. You got no worries baby girl. I'm going to take care of you. I was so sick of hearing that. Everyone that says that seem to have ulterior motives, but I had nothing to lose that night and I needed the break from my reality. I sat back and he put a folded paper to my nose and said inhale deep and hard baby girl. It tasted like aspirin and burned my throat and nose.

I gagged. He laughed and put his tongue down my throat. My body felt so good. I wanted him so bad and nothing else mattered in the world at that moment but getting a nut. I wanted him inside me. I wanted his cum inside me. I needed to feel his dick cum and fill my pussy whole up. I ripped at his jeans, and he lifted me up and carried me to his bed. We rocked and dipped on that waterbed. It was like I was being rocked into the dick. His grind was driving my pussy mad. I pulled him deeper and deeper inside me. He lifted my thighs and began to pound my pussy I felt his dick throbbing. I'm Cumming I screamed he thrusted faster and faster and fell on top of me shaking. I was shaking too, that was the best orgasm I ever had. He looked at me and grabbed

His phone. We need some Chinese after this. I

laughed and agreed. I'm starving like Marvin I said playfully. Can I use your phone? Huh? He said. He pushed another number and told someone to bring him an iPhone with unlimited minutes. I was impressed and I was going to do what it took to keep this going. It wouldn't take long to get on my feet and save my sister. I would give her a life she and I deserved.

John

I wasn't in the business of keeping hoes anymore, but I really liked this little bitty. She was so cute and innocent. Not to mention I could see the hunger in her eyes. She wanted and even needed to come up. I wasn't sure of what fueled that fire, but I would find out. She could be a gold mine. She would be worth having this secret man cave. When I looked at her it was like being 25 all over again. She was so alive I needed that in my life. What else was I to do but help this girl. She would eventually be scooped up by a man anyway why not me? I told myself this, trying to make what I did ok in my mind. I knew that if this was my daughter id lose my cool but the ratchet nigga in me kept living with no remorse. I had debt I needed to get free of and she needed whatever she needed. I would be that man to help her I just would get mines too. It was a win, right? I Knew right from wrong but if they were going to get in some trouble at least I can be there to help. I had big plans for her. I'm not just a small-time pimp. I had clubs and condos and a bad ass guest list. I was all about the money and having a blast while doing it. I was very well connected in the city, so modeling, and any other things the girls fancied id help with. I cared about my women's goals as well as mine. I don't want them feeling sad and dependent only on me. I wanted them to choose me because they liked it. If I could just stay sober and not in her pants, we could make some money together.

Recently my best friend passed away and I wasn't taking it so well. I stayed up drinking and doing lines to numb the pain. My work started to suffer and my social life too. I didn't reach out to my wife because I was positive, she was sleeping around. She had the nerve to be with my cousin at that. When I looked in her eyes, all I saw was lies. I was alone and when my boy brought her here tonight it was heaven sent. This was my chance to turn it all around. I needed to find a way to keep my condo and not take from the joint account that me and my wife shared. I needed her to know nothing about my life. She was a sneaky business partner as far as I was concerned. We were over and I was going to find a way to come up for me and my new lii bitty. Time was money so we were going to get to it.

Latoya

I was sexy, I knew that for sure. I had John go get me some of the best foundation money could buy. None of those horrible bumps and scars were visible. I was so worried about my skin that I decided I'd never do drugs again. At least I could smoke. But nothing white or pill like form unless for pain. This was new leaf for me, and id most definitely use it for good. The scars on my face were a rude awakening. The plan was for us to go to the club and audition to be a dancer, but someone was on the phone with him earlier that shook him and his boys to get their guns out. I was too high at the time to even feel fear or worry. Whoever was on the phone earlier made him terribly upset and scared. He began to make plans to hideout. So, I'm guessing there was no more working for the night. He grabbed my arm and rushed me back to his Condo. He kissed me and told me the place was mine as usual and if I needed anything to help myself. He told me not to open the door for anyone not even his boys. Act as if no one is home doll face. Something may be going on, but I got it under control. His eyes said differently. I grabbed is waste and asked him to stay with me. "You don't have to go. Let's just lay up and fuck. Hide out together. I look too good to just not play around at all." I said it in the sexiest voice I had,

And still No bite. He left in such a hurry he didn't close the safe back. Wrong move I thought to myself. I was worried about him though. I hope he was going to be ok and not do anything crazy to further throw his life away. I did care for him I just already picked up too many habits from him and I have nothing but a few wigs and Jordan's to show for it. I was done being used unless it was for me. First, I needed to call my sister. I knew my cousin and her was thick as thieves, and I could get her cell from her. I had counted out at least $350,000.00 I grabbed out of the safe. I didn't take it all because I wasn't trying to rob him. I just wanted to get off on a good start. Get a trade or degree and a nice house somewhere. I hadn't told anyone, but I knew I was pregnant. So, I was taking enough for my baby as well as me. I was also planning on taking care of my little sister. She and this baby were all I really had now and that's my whole motivation.

I decided to make myself useful. I cleaned up. Turned on the jacuzzi cleaning mode and vacuumed. My plan was to have the house clean for him and his coked-out ass would never even think to count his money. He never did anyway. He just threw the money in and took some out when he needed it.

That was one thing I loved about him. Money didn't matter to him. He worked hard and he spent money freely on whoever was around. My phone started buzzing I looked at it and saw a facetime from John. I answered trying to show off my sexy cleaning wear, but his voice was so shaky and scared like I never heard him before. Baby? I looked and he was bleeding and had been gagged at one point. His eye looked as if it would pop out the socket. Oh my god I said, where are you? I couldn't bear to watch anymore. Tears streamed from my face. "I don't know he said. Crazy ass Lindsey, Paul's wife. had me taken and beat up." What! Why? What does she have to do with you? We were putting on another pussy party. Paul was sleeping with about all the hoes and his wife found out about his ratchet ass. When she called me, I lied to her, and this is what she did to me. She is not to be played with. You need to get out of that hose as fast as you can. Look in the back my old truck is there. Use that and just go before she finds you too. Why would she do that? Because she is looking for a girl named Jessica and Lex. She knows about my place because I threw parties for us all there. Get out! Oh shit! he said and threw the phone. I couldn't see him, but I could hear him. He was begging for his life. Pleading through the beating all I could do was listen. Then a loud thud and it was silent except for a sinister laugh. What the fuck I heard a male say. He looked right into my tear-streaked eyes. Hey lady who are you? I hung up. I must get the fuck out of here. For all I know she saw the fountain in my background and knows where I am now. I had to call my sister because Jessica and Lex are their names? That's no coincidence. I had to warn them. And what was my baby sis doing at a pussy party? I was going to beat her hoe ass. Like seriously, because she knows it's easier ways to get money as smart as she is. I packed a bag of all my favorite things and ran out the door to see what kind of truck this was. I pulled up the tarp and saw an old Tahoe, but it was sexy because it was customized pant and rims to match. Bright blue with red sprinkles in the pain and blue and red rims. The title was in the glove compartment I had won with this one. Life had sent me so much trouble but finally I was beginning to win. I reached for my phone to call my cousin. I knew she would have my sister's number. I was a woman with a mission. Lord help anybody who gets in my way.

John

I knew I was going to die here. There was no way I was getting out of here alive. I had been stabbed and beaten by all of Lindsey's Hench men. Hell, I deserved it. If I'd known all of this would conspire, I'd never planned this party with Paul. He had always been my trouble throughout the years of our friendship. He always there for me when I needed him. He was family to me. He was my brother. I never could see myself getting rid of him because I outgrew him, as so many have said. I kept a low profile and did just enough to get by and saved my money. I had done so well for myself these last couple years, now look at me. I was tied up and bloody in a crazy women's office and as usual Paul had something to do with it. I managed to get my mouth free, and I bit through the tape on my hands. I got my phone out and called my family and Toya to warn her that Lindsey may be on her way to the condo to make sure her revenge was best served. I said goodbye to my kids and gave them the numbers to my safe at my house and the condo so I could die a happy man knowing my wife and kids would be taken care of. I hadn't been the greatest man, but I took care of my family and friends to the best of my ability. I remember when I first met my wife, she was a dancer at V Live. She didn't belong there. You could see that a mile away. She shined as if she was the clubs leading star. She walked on pure air and all the girls wanted her or to be close to her. I made that her last night. From that day forward we were stuck like glue. I loved her more than myself and I made her a happy wife with a good life. I took peace in thinking God may show me mercy because of this. The last words I heard were Toya's my mistress, saying she loved me. Go figure.

Lexi

I needed to locate my sister, but I had no clue where she could be. I could not and would not fail her again, so I was willing to look wherever. But I wasn't sure if the bitch Lindsey was dead or with the police. I had to get out of town. Jessica was scared shitless. We kept going back and forth on rather not to go. I had the money and the deed to the house that I already signed and filled in my name to all appropriate paperwork. I made up my mind and I was leaving by the end of the week. My phone was ringing, and I was in no hurry to answer but the idea of missing my sisters call would kill me. It was my cousin crazy ass and id normally ignore her, but she was the only person who kept tabs on everyone one in my family. Hello, oh my god Lexi I'm so glad you answered I have LaToya on the line hold on ill three way her in. Hello, I heard my sisters voice coming through the phone and it was like heaven. I was so happy to finally just hear her voice. Where are you, I said. I need you to come leave with me. I may be in some shit, but I have more than enough savings to keep us in a lavish lifestyle.

Her wheels were turning in her head because it felt like the longest pause ever. "There is no need to ask what you got into I don't want you talking on the phone. You already said too much. Where can I meet you? If you say you have money, I don't need to go get anything. Just come pick me up. 5178 N 72nd St. I'll be outside waiting for you. She hung up and I was already on my way. I phoned Jessica to make sure she was also ready to go and in place. Neither of our cars we drove were in our names so I assumed we would just drive and follow each other. Jess! I said with excitement loud in the phone. I found my sister! She screamed with the same excitement. That's great because my cousin and his friend are coming too. After the crazy shit with Lindsey, I won't dare go on this journey alone. My boo rides with me and my cousin zander rides with you. And something tells me, you won't mind. You can thank me later.

Whatever bitch gets in place. We are meeting at 5178 N 72nd[th] St. Cool I'll see you in 25 mins. She hung up and I decided to grab us all some goodies from white castles before we hit the road. I pulled in and ordered twenty cheese only burgers and four cheese fries with ketchup. Right as I pulled out my wallet and the cashier complimented my nails a hooded man started shooting. I sped off ducked down swiping the whole side of the building. I hit the corner and called Jessica. Grab Latoya and meet me at the corner of Vandeventer and spencer at the end of the trailer park. Now! I screamed like I was out of my mind and hung up. I could hear the cops in the distance, and I had a fool proof plan. I hated to do it, but I started taking off my perfect Lace front and was about to let my afro out free. I snatched off my wig and put it in my bag. I grabbed all I could and got ready to jump. I hit the gas and right before it went in the lake I jumped out. I took off my dress and wore my Victoria secret shorts and sports bra set. I put the dress in my bag and poured my water bottle all over my hair. I saw Jessica hit the corner and come to a wild turning stop. I ran and hopped in alongside Zander. In the back seat my sister smiling at me. We sped off. As we passed through the intersection, we saw the police cars speed right passed us. To them I looked like I had been swimming and there was no sign of my car. We made it and that gave me hope we could really pull off this plan. I looked over at Zander, he was so dam fine. How was he in this car right now? He was looking at me with my wet hair and white tee shirt like I was a snack. I was willing to be his snack too, but I had to be sure I could trust him. I couldn't just go Gaga over the first fine man I met willing to obviously deal with my bs. "What the hell happened? said Jessica from the front seat. She had a huge scowl on her face as if I started the shooting at the drive thru. I'm not sure I said. I am sure it was Lindsey's men trying to get back at us though. Who in the hack is she? And how did she have so much gangster going on as white as she was? I cleared my mind for a second and turned to get a good long look at my sister. She was a welcome sight. Beautiful as always. I saw her scars from life but right now it was about the loving each other. I'd get to the questions later. "So where are we going?" Here I said handing my phone to Jessica. How do you know they won't find us? Because one thing I know about Paul is that he was very secretive. Lindsey stole his private belongings and savings, but I know she wasn't aware of it all until now and I stole it before she could get to it. I hope your right Jessica said with fear in her voice. I Pity the bitch that come for us baby! Jessica's man spoke up. I rolled my eyes and look over to Vander. He laughed and looked deep in my eyes. I got you baby He said and tapped his belt. He was packing and the way his Nike shorts was looking he was really packing heat. I smiled at him and his teeth were perfect. I knew from our vibe we were going to have some fun. Only time will tell if they are into us for the money and excitement, but I was willing to go for the ride. Only I knew where the money and the house were. I had already put all the funds in an account near the house. I was that bitch.

Latoya

As bad as I wanted to go off my little sister I couldn't. I was so impressed with the way she handled the shooting and the fact she was running the show. I wasn't quite sure What I could say to her. Look at what I was doing. I wanted to ask questions and tell her that Lindsey was not as she seemed. She worked for a powerful cartel. Her father was a drug lord in a gang. They would have a price on her head. I'm sure her and her lil girl toy knew this already after the shooting. Plus, I wasn't sure about the men in this car. I wasn't going to say a word in front of them. I have a child on the way, and I was going to do nothing but win from now on, me and my sister. They had guns I had guns too. If they try it, ill end it. I wanted to at least touch basis with my sister, so we were going to have to stop and eat when we got out of the state. Did she contact our mom? Was there going to be anyone looking for us? I needed answers so I could help in any way possible. I was done sitting back letting little sis ruin her life. More importantly I was a mess. The day I planned to leave my man he calls me on his death bed being killed by the same woman who is now hunting my sister. I had tried to warn john about getting into mess with that man, but he didn't listen.

Rocky aka Paul's bottom chic

I wasn't sure what was going on, but I knew my best friend was in trouble. We spoke at least ten times a day every day and today I have heard nothing from him. He was acting crazy the last time we spoke. He said his wife had been on some wild mob shit. Waving guns and threating people. He wasn't sure if she was on her way to off his little girl toys or if she was on a bigger plot for his personal savings. I've known Lindsey for years and I knew she was a sneaky and involved in something she didn't tell him about. That's why I never felt bad for being his listening ear and shoulder to cry on. I knew everything about Paul. We were together when his wife came in the picture. I couldn't let the hustle go. I was too pretty and making too much money off my cookie to stop and be normal. I wasn't going to stop and both I and Paul agreed on it. Paul was my everything always has been and always will. He will always love me, and I'll always love him. It has nothing to do with the money it our vibe, even though I put him on to all the money. I brought him up in the game. I made him who he was today, and he always said he had me when it was all said and done. In my mind he was my husband. We shared his real life together. His mother can't even know him better than me.

Lindsey was not his type he just wanted that family life and play husband. He was never that type and never a one-woman man. I was on him every day to figure things out and we planned to run away together by the end of this year. So, him not calling or texting was crazy as hell. I could feel it now, something wasn't right. I was going to find my Paul, even if I had to blow up our secret. It wasn't like him not send me messages during the day and at least a goodnight. I was hoping on a plane and heading to his house. Me and Lindsey can have a nice one on one.

No one was stealing my dream home and my money. I helped him save that money. It would be war on anyone who thought about taking what was mine.

Jessica

I was excited and scared as hell. Lexi got us in some shit as usual and this time I wasn't sure her fairy tale will come true. All I knew was, I'm sure the cops were looking for us. If they didn't Have proof, we, did it, they would at least need answers as to why the hell the place is shot up. I had no money and no future in what I was doing or where I was living. I did love Lexi so this was our plan, and now that I have my boyfriend it might be ok. Fact I knew for sure was, it was a chance that I may never make it back alive or if I did, I may be in jail. When I first decided to go for the ride of life, she told me the hustle was real. Neither of us had much to return home for so why not?

We hit the road in our one car, and I was praying that it would be just as we planned it. The issue I had was Latoya knew more than she was telling us. She let out that her sister was playing with fire, and she didn't know who she was messing with. I am going to find the underlying cause of it. if for noting more than to be better equipped for the situation we may be in when we arrive at our so-called house of pleasure. I looked at Lexy and I could tell she was worried, and she had all right to be. There could be someone waiting for us at the house or anything. We were not sure of the Wife's whereabouts or if the police officers were on to us. Lexy said she has a plan rather the house is a go or not, I was her rider and no matter what I was by her side.

Lexy

I sat back in my seat and zoned off. I'm not sure why but I became so relaxed and chilled. I need you right now momma. My new boo thang squeezed my thigh, asked was I ok? Really, I thought in my mind. No way this boy cares anything for me. But I was in a needy, clingy, I need a shoulder to cry on, and great fuck, kind of mood. I looked at his sexy body head to toe and I smiled. I am now I said with a glimmer of naughty in my eyes and biting my bottom lip. He looked at me and said, "can we pull over at the next gas station?" All while keeping his eyes on me. He was sucking my nipples and clit with his eyes. He was so chocolate brown with green eyes. His smile was perfect. With thick juicy lips ready to bite and suck on. His arms were nicely built like he could pick me up and make love to me on a wall with no effort. I looked at him and gave him the look to say I was game. I told Jessica to take us to a Walgreens. I whispered to boo to go into the women's bathroom in ten minutes. I ran to the counter and bought feminine wipes, condoms, makeup, and perfume. I was going to look right. Not like a runaway criminal. I headed to the bathroom and freshened up. I was sexy as hell in the Walgreens bathroom. He opened the door and pulled me to him. He threw me against the door and pulled my pants off. Come here he said. Let daddy make it all better. He lifted me in the air sitting my pussy on his face and my legs wrapped around his neck. Supporting my weight on his shoulders and arms. I screamed out in pleasure. I could not take the pleasure all at once. He slowed up and then faster and faster until I came all in his mouth and lapped it up licking and tongue fucking my pussy. He sat me down and handed me a wipe as he washed off his face. I cannot wait to have all of you doll face he said as he walked out the door. I sat back against the wall, my cookie screaming for the dick with the biggest grin. With all this craziness going on I am in the Walgreen's trying to be nasty. I can only be me and live my life to the fullest. I had a new identity with money in the bank. A house in my name. with a lawyer waiting to speak and meet my new identity and discuss my bonds and money. I was all set. Now that my best friend found us sexy bodyguards, I was starting to believe I could really pull this off. Either way, even if I had to run to get away from danger, I had my bestie and my sister.

I walked to the car with new clothes, and a new attitude. I got in and handed everyone a soda. Let's do this I said, as I looked at the

map. It's a long way to Pawleys Island.